WRITERS REPUBLIC

RED WATSON

AND THE

GIFTED LANDS

L.J. Hardwicke

WRITERS REPUBLIC L.L.C.
515 Summit Ave. Unit R1
Union City, NJ 07087, USA

Website: *www.writersrepublic.com*
Hotline: *1-877-656-6838*
Email: *info@writersrepublic.com*

Ordering Information:
Quantity sales. Special discounts are available on quantity purchases by corporations, associations, and others. For details, contact the publisher at the address above.

Library of Congress Control Number: 2023918266
ISBN-13:   979-8-88810-986-1   [Paperback Edition]
                  979-8-89100-362-0   [Hardback Edition]
                  979-8-88810-987-8   [Digital Edition]

Rev. date: 11/14/2023

For my whole family—for dealing with me.

For my amazing friends—for dealing with me.

And for my crazy cats—again, for dealing with me.

Prologue

The cold stone halls led to a brightly lit area. The light was warm and special—always that clue one needed to find whatever one was looking for.

Needless to say, this was a wondrous place. Though it was a small castle compared to its own green country. There were many beautiful trees, and sunlight passed through their wonderful canopy. As for the castle, it was taller than the tallest mountain, older than the oldest tree.

It was invisible to the human eye, some would say, it was partly true. The royal land would only show its face to people who had faith in its existence.

It was the first home to the first visitors, and at this time, the royal family entered the magnificent abode—the king and his two sons. One son, the eldest, was confident, wise, and kind-hearted. The other was brave and ambitious. Both were honorably kind souls and, at the moment, were preparing for another person's arrival.

"How much longer?" asked the younger son. He was usually impatient and would always have some kind of excuse for anything he did.

"What have we talked about?" said the kind king. "Impatience blinds you."

The younger prince would often be confused by his father's words, but ignoring them would regularly create some sort of disaster. Though he usually didn't understand, the prince tried following his father's ways.

"I remember when I was your age," started the eldest son. "I was just like you—impulsive and immature."

The younger prince glared at his older brother. Their conversations were usually like this.

They soon heard a loud knock, and the eldest prince quickly walked over to the door. Outside stood an old man. He carried a beautifully crafted bow and a quiver full of matching arrows. He swiftly walked over to the king, his face full of worry.

"Mr. Stone, what is the problem?" asked the king.

The old man gently placed the bow on a wooden table. The bow was engraved with a tree of some sort and seemed to be thousands of years old.

"I have foreseen terrible events." Mr. Stone was obviously shaken. "The one who wields this bow shall be our defender against him."

"Against whom?" asked the eldest son.

Mr. Stone was a kind man whom the king trusted very much. But his words were hard to believe, considering no threat had ever passed through the Gifted Lands.

Mr. Stone didn't make eye contact with the king. He feared what would happen if he didn't choose his words correctly.

"I do not know yet," he lied. "You must give this bow to whoever is worthy."

The king frowned. "Is it urgent? I wonder if you fear for nothing, my friend. Though I trust you, I am still unsure of what you're asking for."

"Hide it," said Mr. Stone, "until it is time. Though it could be many years before we find the one who shall be our advocate."

His words were frightening. The king and his sons had never seen their old friend so afraid. He was usually the one telling them not to fear. The younger son smiled; he knew it was him, this person they were talking about. Well, he was not completely sure, but who else could it be?

"Why are you smiling? This is serious," said Mr. Stone. "I assume you won't be smiling if you find your lands in ruin, your people gone."

The younger prince hid behind his father.

"Please, Mr. Stone," said the king.

"I apologize," said Mr. Stone. "What I mean to say is that this is a serious situation. I'm afraid of what will happen once that great threat arrives."

"What threat?" asked the eldest son. He was starting to get skeptical. "Why should we be afraid of something we don't even know about?"

Mr. Stone eyed the family. His eyes filled with fear and knowing. But he didn't want to tell them anything. A deep fear and uncertainty would fall upon the family's shoulders. That was something Mr. Stone never wanted to share.

"Don't doubt me," said Mr. Stone sternly. "I know a lot more than you know, I see a lot more than you see, and I care a lot more than you might think. Trust my instincts, for I am not your downfall."

The eldest son fell quiet and looked down. He didn't dare argue with the old man. No good would come of that.

"So what do we do now?" asked the eldest son.

He wanted to act brave for his family, but he wasn't trained for any kind of threat. No one really was.

This land had always been safe. The kingdom was open to all, even humans. This was not to say that the people who lived in this wondrous town weren't all humans but that there were some who possessed something special.

They had what was known as a gift—given to them so they could accomplish great things in their time. Controlling the weather, growing flowers at will, and healing people are just a few of what this gift holds. No one had ever used the gift for evil. No fear had ever passed through these gates, and there was nothing to fear.

"We must stay hidden," said Mr. Stone quietly.

"Stay hidden?" asked the king rather loudly. "Why should we close our gates now? If there is a threat, won't they become suspicious of our sudden actions?"

"No more questions," said Mr. Stone. "I have warned you all. Now please do as I say. Trust me."

The king nodded. So did the two sons.

Mr. Stone started to walk away, but as he did so, he eyed the younger prince worriedly. After he left, the younger prince's eyes started welling up.

"What's the matter?" asked the eldest son.

"He told me to be careful," said the younger prince.

The eldest prince looked at his brother. The younger prince often acted strange, but this was completely unlike him.

"Yes, he told all of us just now."

"No, no, he just told me. It was like in my head or something," said the younger prince, obviously rattled by the sudden events.

The king and the eldest son shared a glance. The king walked over to his youngest son and placed a hand on his shoulder. "Don't be afraid, my son. I'm sure Mr. Stone was just warning you because you might be our defender."

The young prince looked up at his father with wide eyes. "You really think so?"

The king smiled. "Yes, you are made for great things. Just remember to stay true to your friends and family. I see great power in you. Just make sure you use that power for good, Charles."

Chapter

One

The inside of the carriage was warm and calm. While the subtle rocking had everyone entranced.

It was a long ride from Wales back to London, yet twelve-year-old Red Watson enjoyed every second of it.

Red was a pretty young girl with blue eyes and wavy brown hair. She wore a moss-green cardigan that was made by her mother and brown pants to match her button-up boots.

She loved adventure and valued courage. She also loved watching the vibrant leaves fall from the trees' swaying branches.

A decaying red leaf flew into the carriage and landed on her lap, and she lifted it up to inspect it.

"Lovely," she said thoughtfully while turning it with her fingers.

"It looks sad and tired," said Claire, Red's sister. "I bet the wind was not kind to it."

Claire Watson was a smart girl. She had red hair that was almost always styled into a braid and brown eyes. In contrast to her sister's green cardigan, she wore a blue one.

Red brought the leaf closer to her face. She smiled as she traced the darkened spots, which smelled of aged bog water.

"So it's been on an adventure. Well, that only makes it stronger, I suppose," said Red as she released the leaf back out the window. She watched as it swirled, carried away by the wind.

"I find your perspective odd, but I've gotten used to it by now," said Will, the third of the Watson triplets.

Will Watson was known for his cautious outlook on life. He had wavy auburn hair and brown eyes. For this trip, he wore gray trousers and a long flared tunic.

"Odd?" Red frowned. "There's nothing wrong with that."

The trio had taken a trip to visit their ill grandmother in Wales and was just returning. Finally, they returned to their cozy home in London, which they had fondly named the Watson Tower.

—⁂—

Watson Tower was particularly cold at night but very humid during the day, which was odd since London wasn't exactly a humid place. The stars outside seemed to be always shining ominously bright near Watson Tower. Red enjoyed watching them; they sort of reminded her of dancers gliding across the oasis that was the night sky. She loved how they complimented the trees down below.

Staring at the stars always brought back wonderful memories, especially of her and her siblings. The triplets would be turning thirteen the next day.

Suddenly, a cat jumped onto Red's lap. The Watsons' cat, Charlotte was gray and had tired green eyes. Red started to pet the purring feline, who in return sat down beside her.

"So you've been here for about two, five hours now?" said a voice.

Red quickly turned around, her heart beating fast against her ribcage for a quick second.

"Claire! You scared me." Red exhaled in relief upon seeing her sister.

"Aren't you going to wish us a happy birthday?" asked Claire.

Red stood up, but her legs felt numb from sitting too long, so she sat down in the nearest chair and placed the cat on the floor.

Claire picked up the fidgeting animal. "Red, it's four in the morning. You've been up here for over five hours."

Red yawned. "I guess so." She tried standing up, but her legs felt frozen and feeble. "Why'd you come downstairs?"

Claire replied, "Mother said Char was too loud, so I'll keep her in my room for now."

"Yeah." Red was so tired she had no clue what Claire was going on about.

"Get some sleep. Who knows? Maybe you'll be chosen for the 'annual birthday speech' today," Claire said, and then she started heading back upstairs with Charlotte.

Red went to her room and instantly fell asleep on her cloud-like pillow. Unbeknownst to her, immense clouds of deep gray covered the mountains above. As to what was beneath those clouds, young Red Watson would eventually find out.

—⚍—

"Come on, Red! Get up!" said Mrs. Watson. "It's your birthday. Did you at least get a few hours of sleep?"

Red woke up to the sound of her mum, who quickly raced across her room, looking for her daughter's dress. Red wiped her eyes and then sat up on the edge of her bed.

"Sorry, Mother. I was sitting near the window again. Isn't it a little strange how everything near Watson Tower is . . . *powerful*? Well, I don't know what else to use."

"Never mind that. You need to get dressed," Mrs. Watson said. Then she noticed that Red had lazily slipped on her pale green dress with a laced white apron. "Come downstairs, Red." Mrs. Watson sighed with a smile.

Red loved her birthday. It was a golden memory in her heart so carefully crafted. Yet as she walked down the creaking stairs, she heard nothing but silence.

"Surprise!" yelled Mr. and Mrs. Watson as Red and her siblings came in.

There were decorations everywhere, and Red noticed how tired their parents looked, though both kept a decent job at hiding it. They had also prepared a gift for each of the children.

Red enjoyed the scenery and the delighted expressions on her siblings' faces. She then heard something from outside. The guests were starting to arrive. Red opened the door before someone could knock.

Standing outside was a tall woman wearing a blue dress and a large matching hat that covered most of her face. She wore a large gray dress and a matching tiered cape-jacket topped with a ridiculous amount of jewelry. She also had her hair styled into a braid and wore a huge hat to top it all off.

Standing next to her was a man who Red guessed was the woman's husband. He wore a suit and a boater hat and was a tall man with tired bags under his eyes.

"Good morning," said Red.

The woman and the man didn't answer. They just went inside and greeted Mr. and Mrs. Watson.

That angered Red greatly, but she forcefully hid her annoyance. She turned and noticed that Claire and Will were talking by the window, which was also beautifully decorated.

"Happy birthday, guys!" Red smiled.

"Thanks. You too," said Will. He was carrying a large present, which had been given to him by the two rude guests.

"It's almost time for the speech! I wonder whom Mother will choose." Claire grinned.

It was a tradition for Mrs. Watson to pick a Watson family member's name out of a hat at any birthday celebration to give a quick speech about whomever the birthday was for, even if it was their own.

"Children, this is Lady Christine Willards and her husband, David." Mrs. Watson introduced the newcomers with a smile.

"Nice to meet you," said Red through her teeth.

She wasn't accustomed to disliking people she first met, but something about those people didn't sit right with her. She ignored eye contact with the couple, but only because she spotted something odd outside.

Mrs. Watson called for everyone's attention and then proceeded to lift an upside-down hat into the air so everyone could see.

"Our wonderful tradition has been in our family for many years and will continue to bring us good fortune and prosperity for many more years to come!"

She then reached into the hat and read the folded paper she took from it. Everyone seemed to be holding their breath except for Red and her siblings.

"And the person who will be giving the birthday speech is . . . my daughter Red!"

Red sighed and sheepishly walked toward the front of the room. Her siblings smiled, which was probably a mix of joy and relief.

"Good morning." Red's voice was shaky. "I just wanted to say that I am very grateful for my family and . . ." She peered outside the window, and there it was again!

It was some sort of mysterious figure, like an animal or something. Her curiosity and sense of adventure was strongly urging her to investigate it.

Red slowly walked toward the window to get a better view, and then she clearly saw what it was—a dove. Though it looked peaceful, something about it felt intriguing. Red blinked, and the dove was gone.

She ran outside and looked around, but all she saw were footprints. She wondered why they were human footprints. And that wasn't even the oddest part.

Red decided to follow where the footprints led to.

It was difficult running in the tight shoes that Mrs. Watson had asked her to wear, and the sky started filling with portentous rain clouds. She found it strange since there had been no trace of rain for the whole month.

Red had been running for almost twenty minutes when she decided to sit down on a sizeable stone. She was breathing exceptionally loudly, and she covered her mouth in an attempt to cover the sound she was making. For she was now in the forest that her parents had warned her not to enter.

Red wondered why the footprints were softly glowing and why the glow didn't seem to be fading. She noticed that the footprints stopped at a nearby tree. It almost seemed as if the dove—or perhaps a person—completely disappeared. The forest was unsettling, the bottom of each tree was dead, and there were barely any leaves.

Finally catching her breath, Red stood up. With her legs aching from running, she wobbled over to the nearest tree and placed her hands on it to support herself. She closed her eyes as she tried to stand up properly. After a breath or two, she finally straightened up, her hands still on the tree.

And then she screamed.

Chapter

Two

The dead part of the tree started growing more and more alive by the second. Eventually, the whole tree started growing leaves, each greener than the last. Fluorescent lights ascended toward the sky. The tree was fully healed. Red quickly took her hands off the tree. She slowly started walking backward and then tripped over a stone. She looked around. She was out of breath again, but not from running. Everything seemed blurry, and then all of a sudden, a kind light was all she could see.

—⁂—

"Red!" said a shrill voice.

Red opened her eyes. The wind blew against the trees, creating a swaying pendulum motion. It made her feel incredibly serene, but then memories and questions quickly started flooding back. She saw Will gasping for air, probably from running, even as he continued to call her name.

"Hey! We thought you were dead!" said Claire, looking angry yet relieved.

Red stood up with Claire's help, and then she noticed her siblings' clothes were all torn up. At the bottom of Claire's dress were green stains.

"What happened to your clothes?" Red asked, holding a hand to her head.

"Let's just say the forest wasn't exactly friendly," said Claire. "But it doesn't matter. What happened to you?"

Red gazed down and then glanced up at the tree. She wasn't entirely convinced that she should share her newfound ability with her siblings, but she decided to do so anyway.

"Well, I thought I saw something really interesting, so I decided to find out what it was. After I ran for a while, I was so tired and felt that I needed to sit down, so I tried leaning against this dead tree." Red pointed toward the "magical" tree.

"The . . . tree . . . looks . . . fine," said Will. He was still out of breath, so he paused between each word.

"That's because once I placed my hands on it, it started restoring itself! I don't know how or why or if it was me or the tree, but I don't want to know," said Red, pacing.

Claire and Will stared at the tree and then back at Red. They weren't sure if Red was telling the truth or if their sister was simply crazy. Claire walked over to the tree. She placed a hand on it, but nothing happened.

"Try this dead tree, and close your eyes," said Red, pointing at another dead tree.

Claire walked over to the tree. She looked back at Red and Will, who encouraged her to continue. Claire placed both of her hands onto the tree and then closed her eyes. Nothing happened. She tried again but still nothing. Then Will tried it too, but nothing happened as well.

"Let me show you," said Red, feeling a tad discouraged but still hopeful.

She took a few steps forward, though she was almost scared of the many green eyes around her. Then she dug deep beneath the surface. Her heart beat faster as her mind echoed. An echo was always the hardest to control and even to hear or listen to.

"Wait. I'm not so sure about this," said Red, backing up.

"We'll believe you if you show us," said Will.

Red sighed. She cautiously walked over to the tree. She hesitated, breathing in deeply. Slowly, she placed her right hand on the tree, then her left, and then she closed her eyes. Sure enough, the tree glowed and healed itself. But this time, instead of just green leaves, there were leaves that were orange and red and all sorts of colours.

Red beamed. She felt better this time. But when she turned to look at her siblings, she found them speechless. Will even looked as if he was going to faint.

"How did you do that?" Claire asked, her voice quivering.

"I have no clue," said Red. She looked down at her hands. Nothing seemed out of the ordinary.

She then remembered how strange things were at Watson Tower sometimes.

"Do you guys think I'm the reason behind all the strange occurrences in Watson Tower?" Red asked, turning pale.

For a few moments, everyone was silent, and the sound of the wind rustling through the trees became more apparent. Eventually, it started to lightly sprinkle. Red looked at Claire and Will. Both were still in shock.

"We need to go. It's starting to rain!" Red said.

She started to quickly walk out of the forest. Claire followed, but Will was still motionless.

"Let's go, Will!" Claire yelled.

"I'm sorry. It's just that our sister just restored a tree with her hands!" Will exclaimed.

"Come on!" Claire yelled again.

The trio started running. Everyone felt that their legs were sore, but the unanswered questions and mixed feelings powered their legs. The trees were swaying all around them, as if singing or playing some sort of whimsical instrument. The sky was covered in a blanket of gray clouds, and rain streamed down everyone's faces.

A cold wintery feeling escaped this wild circus of an environment.

As Red looked around, she thought, *This is why Mother and Father forbid us from coming here!*

The siblings heard loud animal screeches that rang in their ears, and they instinctively covered them.

"I can't run anymore!" Will said, panting.

The trio stopped. They were all equally exhausted. The rain was now heavily pouring down, and Red was surprised that there wasn't a flood yet.

The trio found a small cave created by two large boulders piled atop each other.

"We'll be safe in here," said Claire, shivering.

They quickly went inside the small cave. It was cozy, and there was even a couple of wood chunks stacked atop each other in the center. Red figured someone had once made a fire there.

Suddenly, a loud roar echoed from the trees. The trio paused; this was much louder than all the sounds they'd heard in the forest combined.

"What was that?" Will whispered, biting his lip.

"I think we're about to find out," said Red.

The loud roars slowly came closer. Suddenly, the animal came into view. It was a large bear. It looked around, occasionally roaring. Red stared at the bear. Something about it seemed friendly—or even vulnerable. She started getting up, and pain sparked from her legs as she did.

"Red! Are you insane?" Will whispered harshly.

Red ignored him and continued to slowly walk up to the bear. Sensing her, it growled in surprise, and Red took a step back. The bear looked up at her, and she noticed that the animal was wearing a necklace with a moon pendant.

Interesting, Red thought.

Claire and Will stared at their sister. Red was known to have a rather fearless personality, but this was a lot even for her. Red stared at the bear's calm chestnut eyes and noticed the telltale gleam in them.

"Guys, it's alright. She's friendly!" Red smiled.

Claire and Will were hesitant. Eventually, Claire started walking out. Will stared at his sister in disbelief. Claire stood about a foot from the bear. Red couldn't tell if her sister was smiling or not, though her eyes easily expressed her discomfort.

Will climbed out, though he stood a few feet away from the bear, who seemed to be smiling. Then the animal started walking toward two trees. There was a bright light emanating from the center, which the trio believed was a way out of the forest. They shared a smile and started heading toward it.

But before they made their way beyond the trees, they were pulled away.

It was Mr. and Mrs. Watson, though their clothes were filthy and torn.

Apparently, the forest isn't kind to anyone, Red thought.

"Get back!" Mr. Watson yelled to the bear.

"No, Father. The bear was helping us escape the forest!" Red yelled.

The bear was frightened and ran off into the forest. Rain started pouring much more quickly than before, and that same wintery feeling became more intense. Mrs. Watson cleaned the mud and dirt off her children's faces.

"I promise that bear was good. I could feel it." Red's eyes started welling up, half from the rain, half from her tears. "Mother, I'm sorry I didn't listen," she said quietly.

"Never mind that. I'll talk to you once we get home," said Mrs. Watson, hugging her children tightly.

An hour went by, and the rain and everything around them became more intense by the second.

"Red, do you remember your seventh birthday party?" Mr. Watson asked.

Red was confused. She wondered why her father would ask such a question at this time.

"Yes, I remember the lovely cake you made me. It was the most delicious thing I've ever tasted in my life." Red smiled at the thought.

Pretty soon, the rain started to become less heavy and the animal screeches less frequent. They smiled. They weren't sure what was happening, but they were glad everything was starting to get back to normal. As everyone noticed houses starting to come into view, they shared a mutual sigh of relief.

Mrs. Watson opened the door to the house, and it echoed an empty feeling.

"What happened back there?" Will asked.

Red wasn't listening. The entire day was just a blur. She put her hands on her head and lay down. That was when the questions started pouring in.

What happened? Why did Father ask about my seventh birthday? Was all this because of me?

Red's back ached. She could feel and listen to her heartbeat without doing anything. The loud sound, like a drum, started getting quicker and more uncontrollable as she listened.

Then the family heard thunder.

"Red, calm down," said Mrs. Watson.

Red sat up and stared at her mother. *How did she know?* Red thought.

Claire and Will shared the same question.

"What?" asked Claire.

Realizing what she said, Mrs. Watson shook her head. She walked over to the piano in the corner, opened it, and took out a dusty book.

"I'm sorry you had to find out this way," Mrs. Watson said softly.

The thunder started to increase a little. Mr. Watson walked to the window and closed the curtains.

"Tell her quickly, Amelia. The storm has gotten more intense than ever," he said.

Mrs. Watson hesitated, taking a deep breath. Claire and Will were on the edge of their seats. Will looked pale, but that was probably from all the running he did earlier.

Mrs. Watson gave the book to Red, and Red blew the dust off it, which caused everyone to start coughing. She read the cover and then looked up at her parents in disbelief.

Chapter

Three

Red read the cover over and over again.

"*Dealing with Your Gifted Child*?" Red said. "What does that even mean?"

Mrs. Watson sighed. She never thought she would have this conversation with her daughter so soon.

"You're not magic like you were probably wondering. You're just . . ." Mrs. Watson paused as if she was trying to explain something so large in a seemingly small way. "Gifted," she finished.

"What do you mean *gifted*?" Red asked.

Mrs. Watson took a deep breath and explained, "Okay, Red, as far as we know, there are only a handful of people with this talent. I don't want to scare you, but you and your emotions can control . . . well, almost anything. A long time ago, these people's abilities were known throughout this world. But people in power feared that these gifted people would overthrow them. There used to be a lot more gifted people in this world, but now the only ones left are those who escaped."

"But I have no memories of making trees grow or doing anything unusual . . ." Red stopped. "Well, I guess the weather has always been a bit weird around me, but it's always been like that, even when I'm not mad or stressed."

"That's just because you haven't learned to control it yet," said Mrs. Watson.

Red was quiet. She didn't know how to answer.

"Calm down before all of England gets flooded!" Will yelled.

"William!" exclaimed Mrs. Watson.

Red tried to calm down. She placed a hand on her heart to feel her heartbeat. It was racing.

"What's happening?" she asked quietly.

"You have to control your emotions. They can cause destruction," said Mrs. Watson, who hated being this blunt.

Everyone was quiet. Claire and Will started taking a few steps away from Red.

"Why don't people talk about gifted people?" Red heard herself ask Mrs. Watson. "Shouldn't we have heard about it by now?"

"Well, as time passed, people of this world started believing it was just a folktale. Besides, only the people who believe and trust will ever know the true history of the 'gift,'" Mrs. Watson said solemnly.

"Why do you keep saying *this world*?" asked Claire.

"I would never be able to explain everything in a way you all deserve, so let's just calm down for now. I promise you'll get the answers you want soon enough," said Mrs. Watson, purposefully directing her words to Red.

—⟨⟨⟨—

After a few hours, the storm slowly started disappearing. The Watsons were all quiet and tired. Many times, Red had almost started crying, but she would stop herself when she started feeling any strong emotion. But it was extremely hard to not feel *anything*. Mrs. Watson told her she could learn to control her power better so that she wouldn't cause a storm every time she got angry or sad.

Everyone had to change their clothes, considering they had all been drenched in the storm. Red was happy she didn't have to wear the uncomfortable dress anymore.

"What now?" Claire asked.

"You will have to leave," said Mrs. Watson, which was followed by terrified expressions from her children. "I mean," she immediately said, "you three will go together. Your father and I have to stay here to not cause any raised eyebrows. Plus, we're not allowed there anyway."

"But why can't you come with us?" Will asked, his voice trembling. "Surely a few raised eyebrows can't mean that much."

"A gifted person in hiding who last caused suspicion ushered in terrible times for the race. Her whole family was sent to Callum, whom I will not elaborate on."

"The woman's family and many other gifted people were sent to Callum because of one person who had been caught beforehand. Callum promised to spare his life if he told Callum where the other gifted people were hiding. So now a huge population of gifted people are gone," said Mr. Watson. "And Red needs to learn to control her abilities. My sister will help her."

The kids had never really heard much about their introverted aunt, Eleanor. The last time they saw her was probably when they were four, which explained their lack of memories of her. Mrs. Watson had once described her sister-in-law thus: "Great with a sword, not much with any sort of social skill."

"What's so scary about this Callum person? I bet even non-gifted people can overthrow him," said Red.

"I don't want to talk about that right now, Red," said Mrs. Watson sternly.

Red was silent for a moment. "When do we leave?" she asked. "And where do we even go?"

"You will leave in two days, which will give us enough time to tell people that you three will be sent to a correctional facility. Yes, I know that sounds awful, but it's enough to pacify all the questions. And you will be staying with your aunt. She lives in a place called Cuimhne Mountain. To get there, you have to head through the forest again." Then Mrs. Watson turned to both Claire and Will. "And you two better keep Red calm during the whole trip. You'll know her home when you see it. It's an eyesore, in my opinion." She shook her head at the thought.

Will wasn't even listening, and Claire was trying to understand the route. Red felt confident; she was shivering with excitement. But then she realized it was from pure fear.

—◆—

Claire and Will abruptly walked into Red's room. Claire was holding about a dozen books, so Red could barely see her face. Will quickly started pacing around the room, which didn't surprise Red. She was used to this erratic behavior of his.

"Alright, I found these books that I think could explain more about you," said Claire. She threw the books on Red's bed and sat down on a chair next to it.

Will handed Red a book from Claire's pile, and Red read its title.

"By the Order of Callum: All Gifted People Dead." She glared at him.

"Just read it," he said.

Red opened the book.

"Page 27," said Will.

Red turned to the page; it was on chapter 3, "The Origin of Gifted People." The pictures weren't very well drawn, and she cringed at some of them. She noticed something handwritten on the bottom of the page.

Thoir an aire air an staidhre.

"What does it mean?" asked Will.

"It's written in Scottish Gaelic," said Claire. She turned to Red. Do you know what it means?"

"I think it means 'Watch out for the stairs.' But that doesn't make any sense."

"What do we do now?" asked Will. "Please not something dangerous!"

"All we can do right now is go to bed," said Red. "We'll figure something out in the morning."

Both Claire and Will nodded and headed out of the room. Red placed the books on the nearby chair and eventually fell into a deep sleep.

—⁘—

Morning came.

Claire and Will were able to fall asleep but only for only a couple of hours. Red spent the entire night staring out her window. It wasn't the same as the window in the living room, though it still gave her the mindless proactivity to get lost in her thoughts. She was very scared. She noticed it was raining outside—not a coincidence. She wished she wasn't one of the gifted. She started shivering and almost started crying but tried her best not to. Her town had had its fair share of incidents because of her, and she didn't enjoy being the cause of it all.

She closed her eyes and then remembered that she had a lovely dream of a meadow of golden flowers. She was dancing and laughing and was surrounded by her family. It seemed so real.

Suddenly, her siblings came rushing into her room. Red noticed the book Claire was holding. There was a note tucked into it, and she could see it peeking out of the top. The book was about fish, which elicited a disapproving comment from Will.

"I don't think *The Wonders of Ocean Life* will be of any help." His expression quickly changed once he noticed how annoyed his sisters were.

"Read the note. I found this deep in the attic with the other books," said Claire.

Will took the note and read it aloud: "A book titled *The Book of Gifted Memory* can be found in the Watson Library. The book is centuries old and must be held with extreme care. Beware any kind of intruder or guard."

"'Beware any kind of intruder or guard'?" Red echoed. "What do you suppose that means?"

Claire and Will exchanged glances. It was a tough job to distinguish the look of pity in their eyes, for they wanted to help Red discover more about herself, but were scared of what could happen. Red swallowed the lump in her throat and proceeded to check out the book.

"Wait. There's something taped on the back," she said. Then she read the writing out loud.

The book of courage, some call it,

for danger lurks at every doorway.

Beware the trick that guards thy door

and enter at the request of Mr. Wildur.

Do not fear, for the light that shines in all our lives

will save us from a thousand cries.

We all have gifts that we hold,

though "Use them for good," we are told.

Do be careful, do be brave,

for the journey could end a thousand ways.

"It's a poem," said Will. "Well, I guess I'm not sleeping tonight."

"Okay, we can't just rush right in and grab the book," Claire said, looking at Red. "We don't even know where the Watson Library is, and 'Beware the trick that guards thy door' sounds pretty ominous."

"Wait, guys," said Red. "This is in the exact handwriting as that note in Gaelic."

The trio shared worried glances.

"We can't find the book today," said Red. "We don't even know where to start. Besides, we need to wait until Mother and Father are awake so we can ask them where the library is."

Claire was surprised. Usually, her sister would go for any kind of adventure at any time no matter how little evidence she had. Claire was glad yet confounded that her sister was seeing the situation rationally.

Red started reading the poem again to understand it. Will, on the other hand, kept pacing around the room.

"Who in the world is Mr. Wildur?" asked Red.

"Probably a person." Will's remark prompted a look from Red and Claire.

"Mr. Wildur was a friend of your Aunt Eleanor," said Mrs. Watson, entering the room. She had heard the trio's conversation from outside.

"What happened to him?" asked Red.

"I can't recall." Mrs. Watson rubbed her chin. "I don't believe Eleanor fancies that story." She was quiet for a moment. Then she added, "Anyway, children, I expect you all to be packed and ready for tomorrow. You'll be leaving before the sun comes up."

Just as she was about to leave, she looked at the children with a serious face. "Please watch out for the stairs."

The trio was quiet. The colour drained from their faces. Red could feel her heart racing, but instead of being scared, she felt slightly annoyed with herself. Her siblings looked at each other, frantic.

"How did she know?" Will whispered harshly.

"Quiet," Red whispered.

—ɯ—

The trio kept reading the books, trying to find any more information.

Will suddenly stood up. "How long has it been? My eyes are sore! And I think my brain is full. I can't read any longer."

"It's only been ten minutes," said Red.

"Have you guys found anything yet?" Will asked. His voice seemed to go up a few octaves.

Red and Claire shook their heads.

"This is hopeless," said Red. She then remembered the helpful bear. "I wish that bear were here. We need all the help we can get."

"I still don't trust her," said Claire. "She was probably just leading us to her cubs. To them, we're just food."

"Come on, Claire, have some faith," said Red. "I saw the bear had a necklace with a moon pendant. That can't be a coincidence."

"Actually, it could have belonged to the bear's last victim. I bet she's wearing it as a trophy."

"You both sound crazy, you know that?" said Will. "We're all just stressed because it's our last day here. Gosh, when have I ever been the sensible one? That's supposed to be Claire's job!"

"He's right. This is all getting to our heads," said Red, rubbing the back of her neck. "This might sound crazy, but tomorrow we should find that bear. She'll lead us back to the two trees, which might lead us straight to Aunt Eleanor's mansion."

"No, Red. That's too risky," said Claire.

"Listen, Claire," Red insisted, and the rain started pouring slightly harder, "I *know* she's good. I can feel it. I completely believe we can trust her. And trust is the only thing I can rely on now."

Claire and Will looked outside and then at Red. They loved their sister, but they didn't know what would happen if Red became too stressed before they could get to Aunt Eleanor's cottage. They didn't want to find out.

"We trust you," said Claire.

—∿—

The soft rumble of the storm slowly became calmer, though that wasn't enough to eliminate the fear of the coming day. Claire was afraid of Red making something happen with her emotions, Will was afraid of basically everything, and Red was confused, although a part of her felt entranced and enlightened by everything. It felt surreal, but she didn't want to admit it.

Red remembered a line from the poem: "We all have gifts that we all hold, though 'Use them for good,' we are told."

How? Red thought. *How do I use this gift for good? I don't even know how to use it at all.*

She closed her eyes, trying to center herself. She looked up at her siblings.

"We're all given special gifts for a reason, even if it's not a 'gifted' gift. I trust that, and you both should too. We'll figure this out together," she said with a half-smile.

Claire and Will smiled too, and something about this journey became a little less terrifying.

"Red, do you think we should ask Mother and Father about this poem and the Watson Library?" asked Will.

Red looked at Claire. She had the same reluctant expression.

"Let's not worry them," said Red.

"I think that's a little late," said Will, "but I trust you."

Charlotte quickly jumped onto Red's bed. She had a worried expression on her face as she stared at the poem.

"I'll miss you too," said Red, petting the gray cat.

Char meowed and placed a paw on the poem. Her eyes were large, and it was difficult to understand at the moment. She clawed at the poem for a couple of seconds but was eventually pulled away by Red.

"What's she trying to do?" asked Claire.

"I don't know, but she's clearly nervous," said Red, who gently grabbed the cat. "Maybe she just needs some sleep."

The trio stood up and walked out the door. They carried the books to pack later, and Claire carefully hid the poem in one of them.

"We'll be back, Char," she said to the cat.

The gray tabby sat on the bed, staring at the closed door, a look of fear and knowing rested on her face.

Chapter

Five

Morning came, and so did stomach aches of pure fear.

Mrs. Watson walked into Red's room and grabbed the packed bag, which promptly woke Red up.

Red opened the window last night, so the room was freezing cold. It didn't bother her, but she could barely sleep; she kept waking up in the middle of the night.

She had a dream that she was sitting on a park bench, feeding birds, when a flock of more birds came until the whole area was covered with them. She couldn't see where to go and remembered one of the birds even tried talking to her.

The bird had said, "Watch out for the stairs."

Red awoke after that and couldn't sleep the rest of the night. Though she still lay there, wondering why she needed to "watch out for the stairs," whatever that meant.

"Good morning, dear," said Mrs. Watson. Her voice was rigid yet wavering. She was trying her best to hide her sorrow.

Red couldn't make eye contact with her mother, or she wouldn't be able to hold it in. So she sat up and held her pillow close to her. The weather outside was fine for now, and she was trying her best to keep it that way.

"You should start getting up, dear. It's nearly five," said Mrs. Watson. She then handed Red something from her pocket. "And here's a few pounds. Use it only if you need it."

"Thanks," said Red, yawning.

"I'll go wake up your brother and sister. Please get dressed." This time, Mrs. Watson's voice let out a small crack, and she quickly coughed to cover it up.

Red got dressed. She put on the same moss green cardigan and brown pants and slowly waddled out of her room and into the hallway, which was as cold as ice.

In their house, they could always hear everything in the early hours of the morning, like the creaking of the stairs and the first breath of the sun. Red could also hear Will from his room down the hall. He was complaining to Mrs. Watson about getting up so early.

Red chuckled quietly. Waking up early was the least of her worries. Claire opened her door; she was dressed in her blue cardigan and black pants and was carrying her packed bag. She looked exhausted. Red figured she had stayed up all night, reading.

"Morning," said Red.

Claire mumbled something that sounded like "Good morning" and then yawned. She then looked confused.

"Wait. Is it morning already?" she asked.

Red nodded.

Claire quickly ran downstairs. Apparently, that was enough to wake her mind up. Will walked out of his room, and Red noticed that he was shaking. He was clutching his pillow, while Mrs. Watson carried his bag.

Will was wearing his gray trousers with the long flared tunic. He had always hated the cold—and the heat for that matter. Red was never really bothered by the weather; she suspected the reason but didn't want to know anyway.

Claire had packed all the books they were reading the other night; she hid the poem in one of them. Red had also noticed that Claire had rope and flashlights in her bag. Claire was never one to fancy excitement; she enjoyed knowing what was coming next so she could be ready. Red was pretty much the opposite.

However, Red was a bit worried about Will. She remembered all the times she would play outside with her brother and sister when they were younger. Red and Claire loved to climb trees and would persuade their brother to join, but once they were up, Will would be screaming to come down, even when they were only four feet above the ground. Red wasn't sure what Will could handle. Something about the near future seemed ominous, and Red wasn't sure if she liked it. If *she* was feeling this bad, she wondered how Will was doing.

"How do I know if I'm ready?" Red thought out loud.

"There's no way to know that right now," said a voice, Claire's. She was standing behind Red. "I know I'm supposed to be the calm one, but I'm really scared, Red. I have no idea what's going to happen now, and I'm completely terrified." She gazed out the window above the staircase and crossed her arms. "But I remembered a very odd yet amazing person told me to trust in myself and my family." Claire smiled. "Whatever happens, we're in this together, always."

Red smiled at her sister. Her heart felt warm like a fresh batch of Christmas cookies, though she quickly placed a hand over her heart in sudden worry.

"My heart has never raced this fast. It's like that childhood fear that everyone around you can shake except for you. Has it ever been decided whether you should listen to your heart or your mind?"

She took a deep breath and looked to Claire. She lifted her hand from her heart and closed her eyes. She took a minute to breathe the air; it didn't have to be special air to make her feel better. She just wanted to know that a family member was standing right beside her.

"You know what, I think I might be ready," she said.

"I think I am too." Claire smiled.

—∞—

The Watsons were silent. They all gathered downstairs for their last family breakfast. A low storm started outside. Red sighed. She wasn't scared this time; she was more annoyed—mostly at herself. She was still wondering why she couldn't control her feelings.

"Well, if no one's going to talk . . ." Mr. Watson began, "I just wanted to tell you three how proud I am of you all, especially you, Red. I know things are very confusing and scary right now, but I know you three will get through it together."

"Thank you," said Red weakly.

"I let some folks in town know that you guys are leaving for the correctional facility today," said Mr. Watson. "Unfortunately, word travels fast in this town, though now we can use it for good."

"Mother?" asked Red.

"Yes, dear?" answered Mrs. Watson.

"Why was the bear wearing a necklace with a moon pendent?"

Mrs. Watson looked confused. She took an apple and sliced it into three equal pieces. "Well, I don't know. I guess it's possible that the necklace belonged to the bear's last victim."

Red ignored the smug look from Claire. "I just think it's too big of a coincidence."

"Well, it's nothing to worry about if that's what you mean," said Mrs. Watson, "though you should hide if you see that bear on your way to your Aunt Eleanor's house. And stay on the path."

Will looked even more scared. He grabbed his stomach. "Mother, why do Claire and I have to go with Red?"

"I want you all to stay together," said Mrs. Watson. "You're stronger together, you know that?" She checked the time. "I told Eleanor you three would get there by seven. Perhaps it's time to go."

She didn't make eye contact with any of her children. She kept using the "coughing method" to cover up her sniffles or the small cracks in her voice.

"Take this key, Will. It might come in handy," said Mrs. Watson. She handed Will a small golden key, which was shaped like an oak tree.

"Why me?" asked Will. He knew he wasn't the bravest or the smartest. He wasn't sure how he would be useful in this trip.

Mrs. Watson held her son's hands in her own and looked down at his shaking eyes. "You're a lot braver than you give yourself credit for." She smiled.

Will gave his mum a half-smile. He was still confused, but he was also content. He placed the key in his bag.

Red could hear her heart beating a mile a minute. She tried humming to drown it out. That didn't work, so she made her footsteps a tad louder. That instantly caught the attention of Mrs. Watson.

"What's wrong, dear?" Mrs. Watson asked. "I mean about the humming and stomping." She rephrased her question on account of the obvious.

"Sorry. It's just that I want to keep a steady heart rate," Red said quickly.

"I'm so sorry about everything, Red." Mrs. Watson grabbed her daughter's shoulder gently before Red could walk out. Claire and Will stayed as well. Mrs. Watson continued, "I wish you never had this power, but since you do, we need to keep it and you safe."

Red nodded as her eyes welled up with tears. She took a deep breath. She didn't fancy crying, especially in front of other people. She turned to look at her siblings. Will had his eyes closed, while Claire looked at Red and then back at Mrs. Watson. Red knew what she meant, though she struggled to release the trapped words.

"Mother, we found a poem and—"

"Red, you listen to what I'm about to say. You stay safe, and you don't go down the stairs. End of conversation." Mrs. Watson's eyes were large, and her eyebrows were raised. She then walked out of the door in some sort of unrecognizable shadow of guilt and hope.

The trio just stood there, blinking for a couple of minutes. Then they also started heading outside.

The frosty air was a little hard to breathe in, and the mist was blinding. Red's chest hurt as she inhaled through her nose; each breath gave her a small brain freeze. She closed off everything that she was feeling. She didn't think of anything at the moment, so she couldn't care even if she wanted to.

Mrs. Watson smiled. "You three are a lot braver than you think. Remember that." She started tearing up. "We'll see you all real soon, I promise."

Will looked like he was about to cry, while Claire checked her bag to cover her obvious tears.

Red wondered about the dove she saw and why she *had* to follow it. She wondered why *she* out of all people was given a gift and what she was supposed to do with it. Her heart felt heavy, and her feet felt numb. She took a deep breath and then imagined a tree—simple but effective.

Mr. and Mrs. Watson gave the kids hugs.

"Tell my sister we said hello," said Mr. Watson.

"Of course," said Claire. She looked at Red, "I promise we'll keep you safe, Red."

Red smiled. She didn't fancy the idea of her siblings having to keep *her* safe. It made her feel almost jealous, and she envied that her siblings thought she was weak. But that was ridiculous. She quickly buried the feeling.

"Thanks. I think we're ready."

The sun was slowly rising behind the mountains. The beautiful array of colours shone brightly in the vast sky and the seemingly never-ending mist. Hearts were pounding. Some tears flowed, while others stayed in their false places. But the beautiful view escaping from the dull mist was something they all shared.

"It's time for the most terrifying yet amazing journey of our lives." Red looked at Claire and Will. "I'm glad I'm sharing it with you two."

Chapter

Six

For the first couple of minutes, the trio couldn't see where they were going. Every so often, they would bump into a tree, which got irritating fast. When the mist cleared, Red looked around. The first time she was here, she was running, so she never got to see the true beauty of the forest. Seemingly, the trees closer to civilization were much more alive.

"We need to take a break now," said Will. "I have water in my bag."

Red kept looking forward. "Not yet. We haven't even been walking for ten minutes."

She was calm. She knew if she just drowned out all her thoughts, she wouldn't cause anything to happen. She could feel the anger and fear in the pit of her stomach, though it was covered in a camouflaged pile of sand and she didn't dare dig it out.

"This is peaceful." Red smiled.

"I know," said Claire. "You're doing good, Red."

Red exhaled sharply. She didn't understand why she hated Claire's comment so much, but it seemed to burn a little.

The grass in the forest was covered in ice, as were the leaves on the oak trees. Red was also looking out for the bear, unbeknownst to her siblings. But Claire eventually caught her studying the forest.

"You better not be looking for that bear, Red."

"I'm not," said Red, turning her head back so she faced the path again.

The faint animal sounds were a long way away, which was comforting. Red didn't want to start anything; she knew even the smallest misstep or sound could tell animals where the free food was.

"It's funny. I'm sure other thirteen-year-olds are probably reading in their rooms or hanging out with their friends, while we're on this journey to help our gifted sister control her power that she controls with her emotions," Will vented.

"Oh, calm down. It's just another hour and a half till we get to Aunt Eleanor's house," said Red. "You'll survive."

Will grumbled and crossed his arms.

Claire looked around nervously. "Guys, I think I saw something behind those trees back there."

"Stop messing with us, Claire," said Will.

"No, I'm serious! Look!" Claire pointed to the many trees behind them, though there was nothing the competent eye could see. "I promise I saw something."

"I believe you. I'm just glad it's not here right now," said Red. "We don't need a wild animal attack on our list."

"Though you're still looking for that bear," said Claire. "Stop—before you get us killed."

"So I'm the only one who believes the bear is good?" Red asked.

"Yes," Claire and Will said simultaneously.

Red sighed. "Fine. I'll stop looking for her."

The soft wind blew against the trees, which startled the trio.

"It's just wind," said Red.

"What do we do when we get there?" asked Will.

"Well, I guess that's up to Aunt Eleanor." Red smiled.

Claire was silent, looking around the forest anxiously. "Guys, I saw something again."

"Where?" asked Red.

Claire pointed to a group of trees in front of them, where a soft growl sounded. "See!" she exclaimed. "I told you."

The trio stopped.

"Don't move," whispered Red.

The growl got louder. Suddenly, the bear they had seen last time slowly crawled out from behind the trees. The trio tensed up. Then Red slowly started walking toward the bear.

"Red!" Will whispered harshly.

The bear sat down and looked directly at Red.

"I think she wants us to follow her," said Red.

"No, we are *not* following the wild animal. Will?" said Claire, who then looked at her brother, waiting for him to agree with her.

"She's right. We're not following her," said Will.

The bear growled softly and then stood up.

"She just said, 'Follow me,'" said Red.

"Red, how can you understand a bear?" asked Claire.

Red looked back at the bear. "I don't know. Just another question for Aunt Eleanor, I suppose," she said almost reluctantly.

"What's she saying now?" said Will after the bear growled.

"She really wants us to follow her," said Red. "I think we should. Please trust me."

Claire and Will shared a hesitant look.

"Okay, bear. Where now?" asked Claire.

The bear started walking off the path.

"Wait, Mother said we should stay on the path," said Will.

Red and Claire ignored him and continued to follow the bear. Occasionally, the trio would hear a loud screech or roar from a random animal in the woods, though the bear didn't seem bothered by anything.

The bear apparently knew her way around the forest. She would weave through multiple trees, so the trio sometimes had to run to catch up. The bear would not take her eyes off the route even when Will complained.

"That bear's pretty focused," said Red, out of breath. "At this rate, we'll get to Aunt Eleanor's house in a half hour."

Claire and Will groaned.

"I still have second thoughts about this, Red," said Claire.

—ന്ന—

After a while, Will kept complaining about the weather and then about the bugs. Red and Claire had stopped listening to him a while back.

The bear was still laser focused on the path.

"Are you completely sure this bear knows where Aunt Eleanor's house is?" asked Will.

"Positive. Remember, just trust," said Red.

The bear suddenly turned a sharp right. Claire bumped into Will, who then bumped into Red, who ended up tripping over a rock. They all fell into a large bush with sharp thorns.

"Sorry," Claire said sheepishly.

Red and Will glared at her and then got up from the bush. Some thorns were attached to their clothes, so the trio had to wait a couple of minutes to take them out. The bear waited, though it looked almost impatient.

Another growl escaped from behind the trees. Another bear came out, but this one had two scars over his left eye and looked a lot more intimidating. The animal looked at the trio and the bear with the moon pendant and growled.

The bear with the moon pendant immediately stood in front of the trio and growled firmly at them.

"She said to run that way until we see Aunt Eleanor's house!" said Red, pointing north.

The trio started running. Red stopped and looked back at the bears. She wanted to help.

"Red! Run!" yelled Claire.

Red followed her siblings. She felt something on her face. It was blood. The thorn bush probably got her there when she had fallen in. Red ignored it and kept running.

"Almost there! I see something!" said Claire. "It's Aunt Eleanor's mansion!"

Red stopped without knowing. She was in awe. Her Aunt Eleanor's house was really a mansion.

"Red!" said Claire.

Red started running again. She heard the faint cry of the bears from behind her.

She wished she could help. She thought she could maybe do something with her powers, though she knew all she could do right now was trust. Guilt started pouring down rapidly into the pit of her stomach.

Chapter

Seven

The trio made their way to the front of the mansion. They all stood in awe of the grand home. There was a large garden full of all kinds of flowers at the right side of the mansion. It was beautiful, and Red wondered why her Mother hated this abode.

Aunt Eleanor had probably fixed this place up, she thought.

Suddenly, two large doors opened, and a woman walked outside.

"Aunt Eleanor!" cried the kids.

"Why, hello, children! I am so happy you got here safe," said Eleanor. "*Crivvens!* You've all gotten so big since the last time I saw you!"

Eleanor Watson was born in Edinburgh and would occasionally speak Gaelic to the children whether they understood or not. She was an older woman but looked young. Her golden-brown hair was wrapped around her head, complemented with a crown of flowers. She wore a soft-green highland dress, which was also covered in flowers.

Unexpectedly, at that moment, the bear with the moon pendant suddenly ran toward them. Surprised, the trio ran behind Eleanor in shock, though their aunt didn't seem worried. The bear closed her eyes and, amazingly, turned into a girl of about thirteen. She had pale skin, which at the moment had a few scars, and curly black hair. She wore a black dress and gray sweater. And around her neck was the necklace with the moon pendant.

"*Na biodh eagal ort!* Don't be afraid! I see you've met Bailey. She didn't mean to scare you, children."

Bailey half-smiled. "Good morning."

Red thought Bailey seemed odd—kind but odd—like a girl who hadn't seen any human being other than Red's aunt before. She wondered if that was the case for this girl.

Claire and Will were shocked.

"How did you turn into a bear?" yelled Will.

"That's a story for another time, dear." Eleanor also gave a quick half-smile.

"Shall I show them their rooms?" said Bailey with little enthusiasm.

"Oh, that would be lovely, yes," said Eleanor, who gestured to the trio to come inside.

The inside of the mansion was even better than the outside. There was a huge fireplace and many books alongside the walls beside it. A small table rested between many sofas and chairs. A tea set was placed neatly on the table, and a plate with many scones and fudge-looking treats on a platter sat in the center.

Red picked one up in curiosity.

"Ah, my homemade Scottish tablets." Eleanor had a look of pride on her face. "Try them. They're sweeter than fudge."

Red took a bite, and her eyes brightened. She took another, and Claire and Will each took one as well.

The trio was in awe about everything in the mansion. Bailey took their sweaters and coats and placed them on a nearby rack. Will wondered if she ever smiled.

"Of course, I have," said Bailey.

Will tensed up.

"Was that another power?" Claire asked, while Will took a few counted steps back.

"No, your friend here mumbled it under his breath," said Bailey, gesturing toward Will, who laughed sheepishly. "Follow me, and don't get lost," said Bailey austerely.

The trio followed Bailey. There were many turns and it was hard to keep track of the nimble girl. Finally, they reached a floor with many rooms.

"This is your room," Bailey said to Red and Claire.

The room was large and had two beds, one on each side of it. Red figured Eleanor decorated the rooms considering one side had a couple of swords mounted on the wall that had once belonged to past family members and the other had many old books neatly organized into a bookshelf.

They then moved on to the next room, which was Will's. It was pretty much decorated like the entry of the mansion. Eleanor knew Will liked comfort, so this made sense.

"This is my room, and your Aunt Eleanor's is just down the hall," said Bailey. "Take this time to check out your rooms. Meet us downstairs for dinner."

She walked toward the door. She seemed to walk so lightly that you could barely hear her footsteps. Red found that rather odd considering she could turn into a large loud bear. As another wave of guilt washed down, Red held her stomach. She hadn't even said thank you to Bailey for saving her and her siblings.

She held her breath, waiting for the moment to pass, yet she was still there with her mind. And the mind never enjoys sitting still. Red wondered if everyone's mind was like that. She longed for security in the form of distractions.

She decided to read the words engraved below each mounted sword.

"Hey, Claire! This sword is over five hundred years old!" said Red excitedly.

Claire didn't care. She was too busy checking out all the books she had. "Can you believe how many books Aunt Eleanor has?" There was a ladder to reach the books on the top shelf, and Claire climbed it. "There has to be at least eight hundred books here!"

When it was nearly dinnertime, Red was still obsessing over the different swords. There were knightly swords, longswords, rapier swords, basket-hilted swords, and much more, each unique with plenty of battle scars. Claire was in the middle of *Adventures of Huckleberry Finn*; her eyes glued onto each page. She had barely finished *The Fellowship of the Ring*, which had just been published earlier in the year.

Bailey suddenly appeared from behind them, making Red and Claire jump in surprise.

"Ms. Eleanor asks for your presence," she said quietly.

A little intimidated, Red and Claire slowly walked out. The trio walked down the long elegant staircase. The handrail had little designs—oak trees along the border. The sound of the fireplace was very relaxing. Eleanor decorated the long dining table, which also had an oak tree candle as the centerpiece.

"This family really loves oak trees," said Red.

Eleanor laughed. "*Tha*, us Watsons are known for it."

There were small candles on each side, and on the wall was a large window with stained glass.

"Please sit," said Eleanor.

The trio noticed she kept glancing out the window, like she was afraid of something.

"Is everything alright?" Claire asked.

"Yes, of course," said Eleanor quickly. "Just waiting for the post to come, that's all."

The children were silent.

The food Eleanor made was amazing, and Red thought she must have spent a lot of time on it. There was a plate of haggis for everyone, which was the only thing the trio wouldn't touch, but they all kept smiling faces for their aunt.

There was a soup called *tattie drottle*, which was made with potatoes, milk, and onions. Red felt this was her favourite. As for dessert, there was a pudding called *sticky toffee pudding* made with vanilla ice cream.

Bailey joined the table. She had no expression as she ate. The trio watched her intently. Red didn't want to admit it, but she liked the bear Bailey more than the grumpy human Bailey. But it was only the first day, and Red didn't want to deal with any more conflicted feelings.

Eleanor stood up. "Listen, I am extremely grateful that you three made it here safely. It will be wonderful having extra company. Bailey and I haven't seen anybody else in a while. I just have one rule." She paused, looking directly at Red. "This home only has two floors. If you find stairs that go down even further than the first floor, do *not* go down. Ever," she said with a serious expression.

"Yes," the trio said quietly.

Eleanor suddenly went back to her joyful self. "We have many rooms here that you three might enjoy. There's also a library down the hall if any of you want to check that out. Just be careful there."

Red looked at her siblings. Apparently, they were thinking the same thing.

"Do you call it anything else than 'the library'?" said Will, who then got a few glares from Red and Claire.

"What a rather interesting thing to ask, dear." Eleanor laughed softly. "But I suppose it would be our own Watson Library."

"Watson Library," Red repeated.

Eleanor eyed Red. "Have you heard of that name before, dear?"

Red forced a smile. "No, no, I haven't. Sorry."

Everyone was quiet, though it seemed as if Bailey was enjoying the awkwardness.

"If you want to visit the library, don't go alone. It messes with your mind, and you'll be stuck there forever. It doesn't do it to everyone, but you should still be careful," said Eleanor.

"What?" the trio asked simultaneously.

"Never mind that. It's just a warning. Forget I said anything."

A few minutes passed. Everything was still quiet. The crackling sound from the fire seemed to get louder. It was an almost intimidating roar—almost.

"Red, have you ever wanted to learn how to use a bow and arrows?" Eleanor said, changing the subject.

"Yes, I have," said Red excitedly.

Eleanor smiled. "Someday, it might become useful. You never know."

Red noticed that Will was shaking. She wondered why he was always nervous, though she couldn't really blame him after the day they'd had.

"Don't be afraid, Will. Fear doesn't help you," she said calmly.

"How do you just stop fear?" asked Will quietly.

Red became quiet. She wasn't really sure how to answer that question—which was, unbeknownst to her stubborn self, also a question she desperately wanted an answer to.

"I understand, Will." Eleanor half-smiled. "That's a pretty hard question to answer. But remember, you're not alone and never will be. You know, Will, fear is like this candle here." She picked up one of her oak tree candles. "The longer you supply your fear, the less courage you have. Don't ever let your fear win. However, sometimes it can be used as an advantage. I have always admired courage more than bravery."

"Thanks," said Will with a genuine smile.

Eleanor glanced out the window again. Red looked out the window too, but she didn't see anything *that* suspicious. She noticed there was another garden outside, though this one had vegetables, not flowers. Red spotted something unusual about the vegetables. They were all rotten.

"Aunt Eleanor?" asked Red. "What happened to your garden?"

Eleanor looked outside, at the garden. She had a solemn expression yet didn't seem too surprised.

"Callum."

Eleanor looked at the kids and then quickly turned away.

"Children, Callum is definitely someone not to be messed with."

Eleanor glanced at her wall, and Red noticed she was looking at an old painting of two young kids.

"I'm not making that mistake again," she declared solemnly.

Everyone was quiet. Red didn't know if she should talk or just wait until her aunt did. She took another cautious glance at the painting, and it made her feel uneasy. She lowered her head, apparently on cue since the others did as well. Now the question lay still beyond the rusty gates of a memory. What was going on in Eleanor's mind?

Everything was cold and still. Or at least it felt like it.

The sudden tense feeling in the air was enough to throw everyone off track. Eleanor lifted her head with a slight twitch.

"You three can explore for now. Tomorrow, we'll work on archery, Red," said Eleanor, apparently now out of her trance.

The trio headed down the hall toward the library. Claire brought the book with the poem inside it, though she kept it hidden. The entry doors to the library were very large and wonderfully crafted. An enormous oak tree was carved into the doors, and the branches reached out to all sides. It seemed so lifelike.

The trio opened the door. The library was colossal. Thousands of books were arranged in hundreds of bookshelves. There were many pillars, vines grew around them, and a few cobwebs were spotted in some places. The room smelled of cinnamon and flowers, and in the center of everything was an oak tree, over twenty feet tall.

"I didn't know her mansion was this large," said Red, still in awe. She wondered why Eleanor never used the library. It probably had something to do with that "messing with your mind" thing she was talking about earlier.

Claire and Will were silent. Red even thought Claire was crying a little.

"I see the books are labeled alphabetically. That must have taken her some time. Go to *W*. We need a book on Mr. Wildur," said Red.

A few moments later, Will called out, "Over here!" He was standing next to a huge bookshelf with a large *W* carved into the side.

Red and Claire stared at the shelf. It would take them an eternity to find the right book.

"Well, I guess we better start searching," Claire said giddily.

After more than twenty minutes, the trio still hadn't found anything. Will found books on weird gifted animals, and Claire kept getting distracted everytime she found a mysterious educational book.

They were about to give up when Red spotted a dark green book titled *Arthur Wildur*.

"I found it!" said Red.

She grabbed the book and placed it on a nearby table. She wasn't sure which chapter to go to, though one seemed more interesting than the others. She started reading it aloud.

As a young boy, Arthur Wildur had always been fascinated with gifted people. He had continually wanted to study them. He then met a two gifted people, and those friendships helped him see the beauty of differences and, most of all, trust.

"That's all good information, but we need to find something about a request," said Claire.

Red skipped a couple pages. She found a paragraph labeled "Wildur's Request."

"Here it is." Red then started reading the paragraph.

The famous Arthur's request came to be when, in the middle of a battle between the people and Callum, Arthur walked right up to the Treacherous Prince and said calmly, "All I request is the peace and trust of our peoples, which now should and always will shine down upon our hearts."

Some thought the event was unnecessary or pointless, though others believed that this act of courage was what saved them. Since the battle, Callum lost his abilities, though one touch of the book titled The Book of Gifted Memory *will restore his terrifying power.*

"Wow, that's a lot," said Claire quietly. "I now see why everyone's so afraid of him."

Red and Will nodded in agreement.

"So to enter Watson Library, we need to say his request to whatever guards it. Sounds easy enough," said Red.

"I don't know. The poem made this 'trick' sound pretty terrifying," said Will, still staring at the open book.

"This book could explain so much to us, even the backstory behind the gift."

Claire and Will nodded almost unwillingly.

"We still need to find these stairs," said Claire.

"We'll split up. If you find something, let us know quickly," said Red.

She took off toward an area with a large waterfall. There were many books on classic tales and adventures. Claire decided to venture toward an area filled with history books. Will wasn't sure where he was. He just started running in a random direction and got lost.

"Alright, remember what Red always says. 'Just trust,'" Will mumbled to himself.

He noticed that the books seemed to get older as he kept walking. Each cover became more and more faded and broken in some way. Just as he tried to turn around, he saw something interesting—a large painting of a lock on a door. The lock was oddly shaped, and Will wasn't sure what it was.

"I'm going to need a key," he said.

Then he remembered the key his mother gave him before they left. "Of course!" He stumbled to grab his bag and took out the golden key.

He hesitated at first but then slowly used the key. The key seemed to be a perfect match. At first, nothing happened. Then a muffled rumble resounded from below. Will jumped, and he quickly stuffed the key back in his bag.

"Good thing nothing bad happened," he said, sighing with relief.

Then out of nowhere, he was gone, taken by something—or someone—from the opened door. Not a scream could be heard, and all that was left were faint scratch marks on the wooden floor.

Chapter

Eight

Red and Claire searched for many hours. They finally decided to stop looking. Claire found Red at the waterfall, though Will was nowhere to be found.

"You think something happened?" asked Claire, looking around frantically.

"Calm down. He's probably just lost," said Red, though that didn't help Claire calm down.

"Lost?" said Claire.

"It's better than dead. Trust me. He's alright. We'll start looking for him."

Red and Claire started to call Will's name. No answer. They started walking toward the section with the older books.

"These books must be hundreds of years old," said Claire.

"And it looks like he was here," said Red. She picked up Will's bag, which had fallen onto the ground, the golden key still inside.

"Will's key?" Red asked.

"It probably has something to do with that," said Claire, pointing at the painting.

Red took a step back and saw the whole painting of the wooden door. She tried unlocking the painting with the key. They waited a couple of minutes for something to happen.

"Red, Will wouldn't go into a creepy painting like this alone. Actually, he wouldn't go into anywhere creepy with us either. So maybe he didn't go in here. Maybe he was—" Claire stopped and looked at Red. Both their eyes widened in horror.

"Hide!" said Red. She grabbed Claire's arm and pulled her behind a large bookshelf.

The painting opened slowly.

Red and Claire held on to their breaths, not making a sound. They waited for minutes, though nothing happened. Red stood up and then walked toward the painting.

"Red! Get back here!" said Claire.

Red ignored her. There was a large staircase leading down. She stared at it, not sure what to do.

"Claire, we need to go down these stairs. Will's down there."

Claire nodded and half-heartedly walked toward the painting.

"For Will," said Red.

"For Will," Claire said back.

Their teeth chattering from the sudden cold air, they started down the long staircase. Both were shaking with fear. They had many questions, though nothing compared to the question of what they would find.

It took a while for Red and Claire to get to the bottom of the stairs. There were lanterns on the wall beside them.

"Try not to make any sound," whispered Red. Claire nodded.

At the bottom of the stairs, there was a wooden door. Red walked over to the door and tried opening it. It was locked. She had left the key in the painting. But then she saw that there was no keyhole in the door, so the key wouldn't have worked anyway.

"'All I request is the peace and trust of our peoples, which now should and always will shine down upon our hearts,'" said Red, remembering Arthur's request.

Red and Claire stood still for a few minutes. The wooden door suddenly opened, and there stood a tall man. He wore a black coat and had frizzy gray hair.

"Good evening," said the man.

"Hello," Red said slowly. "Who are you?"

"I am the butler of this household. Michael is my name. I see you've unlocked the door with Arthur's request."

He walked deeper into the room. It was a large room (not as large as the Watson Library). There were some books on the floor and an empty bookshelf.

At the center of the room stood a pedestal with a large crimson book sitting on it. The title of the book, in majestic golden letters, was *The*

Book of Gifted Memory. And in the corner stood a terrified Will, who Red noticed had a few burns on his hands.

"Will, are you alright?" asked Red.

"He's fine. I asked a favor from him, though I found that he wasn't gifted,'" said Michael. "I have always been fond of gifted folk, and I wanted to learn more about them. I can't take the only research book from the pedestal. It has some sort of protection trap that burns anyone trying to touch it who isn't gifted."

"Aunt Eleanor never mentioned a butler," said Red, eyeing Michael suspiciously.

"She doesn't like to speak of me. It might be because she locked me in here when she stole my abilities from me," said Michael. "You don't know your aunt that well. Don't give her your trust."

Red and Claire shared worried glances.

"Aunt Eleanor wouldn't do that," said Red.

"Well, she must have told you not to go down the stairs," Michael said. "She didn't want you to find out."

Red and Claire were quiet. They didn't know what to say. Will was still in the corner, terrified.

"How much do we really know about Aunt Eleanor?" Claire's voice was reluctant but steady.

That was true. Red did not know much about her aunt. Only small memories would come to her every now and then, though those memories wouldn't last long.

She turned toward Michael. "Who are you to speak that way about my aunt?"

"All I'm saying is that she can't be trusted," said Michael. "Who can really be trusted anyway? It's just weakness. The human mind is like the weather. You can never truly predict it."

"If what you say is true, then how do we know we can trust you?" asked Red.

"What is trust anyway?" asked Michael.

The room became deadly silent, and Will's shaky breathing became apparent.

Michael pointed at the book. "This book can change everything. Any problem, a solution instantly appears."

"That's not possible," said Claire.

"Really," said Michael. "That's what you think." He stared at the book. "You all have no idea what possible means, not a clue."

Red looked at Michael. "We're leaving now." She quickly ran toward the door. Claire and Will followed.

"The book!" yelled Michael. He tried running out of the room, but some sort of barrier stopped him.

The trio ran up the flight of stairs. Their legs ached. Red's eyes were red and sore. Once they got up the stairs, the trio quickly closed the painting and then collapsed on the floor in exhaustion.

"I'm sorry," said Red. "This is all because of me. You should have no part in this."

"Red," Claire started, "this is not your fault. You were given this gift for a reason. And remember, we'll always be here just until the light gets brighter."

Red smiled. She drowned out everything—the fear, the worry. She was certain that she was going to be okay. Though she didn't have any proof, she still trusted, and she would continue to trust no matter what happened to her.

—∿—

The trio sat around the large fireplace. Claire had a random book in her hand, while Red and Will held a cup of tea made by Eleanor.

"Crivvens, that's some story," said Eleanor after Red explained everything that happened.

"It's all true," said Red. Her teacup burned her lip.

"I know, dear. I wanted to tell you, but I didn't want you to be afraid."

"Why did you even let us go inside the library?" asked Will. He wouldn't make eye contact with anyone.

"The Watson Library is a special place. It's full of wonder and hope. I trusted you all to listen to my warning."

"Sorry," said Red quietly. "Who is Michael anyway?"

"*An Uilebheist sin*! Of course, he would use the name Michael," said Eleanor. "That was my husband's name." She looked away for a few minutes. "He knew that would make me angry." She stood up, then handed Claire a cup of tea.

"He's Callum,'" said Red, her eyes growing wide, "isn't he?"

Eleanor sat down again and sighed.

"Yes." Her eyes looked tired. "You wish to know the origin of Callum?" she said slowly, almost in a trance.

"Yes," they said.

"He was once like you and me, Red, given this wondrous power—a power that should only be used for the good of others. It might be hard to believe, but as a child, Callum was exceptionally kind. I'm not sure if you know, but this power can either bring you joy and hope or blind your heart. Callum was overconfident. He took advantage of his power and soon gave in to the fear. That's is what turned him into what he is today. When I was young, my friend and I contained him."

Eleanor took a sip of tea.

"We just took away his power. He is trapped here because my mansion is one of the safest places I know. *The Book of Gifted Memory* is in the same room as he is, though he can't hold it or even touch it. Only people who have this gift of ours can handle the book, and people with a power like Bailey can only hold the book for about a minute before it burns their hands. All Callum needs to do is get handed the book. Then he will regain his freedom from the mansion and will quickly start regaining his terrible power."

"Terrible power?" asked Claire.

"Yes, he has strayed far from the path, though I fear he might be stronger than me."

"Stronger than us, you mean?" asked Red.

"No, stronger than me. I see a great power in you that I haven't seen since I was young. It might be even more powerful than Callum's if you allow it," Eleanor said softly.

Red closed her eyes. She had many unanswered questions.

"Why didn't you help me control my gift when I was young?"

"That's simple. You weren't ready. I feared that if you knew you had this gift at such a young age, it would be harder to control."

"We'll be here to help her," said Will.

Red looked over at her brother. She smiled, though she was also shocked that he showed a sudden act of bravery. Red was learning a lot about her siblings. She might not want to admit it, but she knew she couldn't do any of this alone. It wasn't a question of whether it was her heart or her mind this time.

Red suddenly remembered her birthday party, the mysterious dove and how she had to follow it. She decided to ask Eleanor. She told her about the party and the dove.

Eleanor smiled. "Interesting. You met one of my old friends," she said coolly.

The children faced their aunt in confusion, Red most of all.

"Who are they?" she asked.

"He's an old friend of the woods. His eloquence defines serenity. He rarely comes out, though only for reasons nobody has yet understood. He's like a grandfather to me and is to everyone else. He is the kindest soul I've ever met."

As the children listened to Eleanor speak, they couldn't help but smile. Then Red looked around the room in question.

"Aunt Eleanor?" she asked. "Where's Bailey?"

"She said she heard something down the hall. It was probably you three, though it's been a while. I wonder where she is," said Eleanor, eyeing the room in confusion.

The trio was silent for a few moments.

"Red, do you have the key?" Claire asked.

Red checked her pockets. "I don't have it. I left it in the painting." She quickly stood up. "This isn't good."

She ran toward the Watson Library. Both doors were locked. Her hands became sore after many attempts to pry them open.

Claire, Will, and Eleanor ran toward the library as well.

"What is going on?" asked Eleanor.

"We left the golden key in the painting, and Bailey has been missing for hours," said Red. She had to take a short break to catch her breath.

Everyone's eyes widened. They exchanged looks of worry.

"What do we do?" asked Claire.

"Find a way to open these doors!"

They each pulled the doors with all their strength, but it wouldn't budge.

"Two gifted people, and you can't even open two locked doors?" said Will, pausing to catch his breath.

"Why did Mother even give me the key? It's almost like she wanted us to find Callum." Will sat down.

He was soon joined by Eleanor, who looked at him solemnly.

"I never told your mum Callum was there. She wanted you to find the book—to protect it."

"What? Why me?" Will asked.

"Your mother has never really trusted me. Her view on gifted folk was tough at first until she had Red, which was why I was so surprised that she allowed you three to stay with me, of all people. She thought you would be the better choice to protect the book than me. I'm starting to believe her."

"No, she's wrong," Will started. "And that room is the best place to keep the book anyway. It's protected."

"Not for long. The book has grown stronger." Eleanor looked at Will, her eyes wide. She then looked at Red and whispered to Will, "Don't tell your sister, but I believe her presence is what's causing the book to act this way."

"That's not possible," whispered Will.

"Will, your sister and I are gifted. Bailey can turn into a bear as she pleases. I'm sure you had a different definition of *possible* before you came here."

Red and Claire kept attempting to open the locked doors.

"This is hopeless." Claire sighed.

"I have an idea," said Eleanor, standing up. "Red, stand in front of the doors."

Red walked over to her.

Eleanor instructed, "Place your hands on the door and close your eyes. Find as much positive energy as you can. Think of a nice memory."

Red breathed quietly. She tried hard to think of a nice memory, but something was stopping her.

"It's not letting me," she said.

"You're not letting yourself, Red. You have to let all your fear wash away," said Eleanor calmly.

Red closed her eyes, and she tried to think of nature. When she was younger, Mrs. and Mr. Watson took the kids on a trip to see Lake Windermere. Though it had been a simple trip, it still brought joy to the young children. Red remembered the endless splash of water, how it sounded and felt. The mist above them was damp and cold. Red smiled. She remembered her family laughing. That was what truly made this memory a happy one.

"Something's happening," whispered Will.

Red's hands were placed on the two doors, which slowly started to open. Like large stone walls or walls of strong iron, it dawdled to open. Though it soon came to a stop, Red heard cries of joy behind her. They ran inside, toward the section with the older books. After minutes that felt like hours, they soon made it to the painting. It was wide open, with the key still in it.

"She went inside," said Red, winded.

Eleanor gazed down the troubling staircase. "I promised myself I'd never go down these stairs for any reason."

Red placed a comforting hand on her aunt's shoulder. "This is a pretty good reason."

Red was the first person down the stairs, followed by Eleanor, Claire, and Will. Each step was loud. They all waited for something to happen, and the deafening silence endured.

"You think she'll be alright?" asked Will. "I mean, she can turn into bear if she needs to, right?"

"*Deas*. Right," said Eleanor, though her voice trailed off into uncertainty.

"Just a few more steps," said Red quietly.

They soon made it to the bottom. Red quickly recited Arthur's request. Eleanor placed a hand on her heart, though her eyes were oddly unreadable.

The door opened with a loud creaking sound, which was soon replaced by quiet crying. Bailey was on the floor, her hands covering her eyes.

"What happened?" asked Red. She ran over to help her up.

"I'm sorry," said Bailey, each word faltering. "I gave it to him."

Red looked over at the center of the room. *The Book of Gifted Memory* was gone. All that was left was an area of built-up dust surrounding the pillar.

"Why would you do that?"

"He tricked me," said Bailey quietly. "He told me Mrs. Watson was his sister and that she wanted the book, so I should give it to him. I wouldn't believe that now, but it's weird how believable it was then."

Red placed a hand on her head and sighed. "It's not your fault." She turned to face Eleanor. "We need to find that book."

Eleanor was lost in thought. She glanced around the room.

"How? He has the book. He must be hundreds of miles away by now," whispered Will. "And even if we did find him, what would we do? Start a rainstorm? You haven't even learned to control your gift yet. There are innocent people out there. You think he would show them any quarter?"

"Do we even have a choice?" said Red. "This is our fault. It is our responsibility to find him. I don't know how yet, but we will find a way to defeat him."

"You sound so confident," mumbled Will, "but you don't even have the slightest idea how to find him. Red, I might be the one who's always afraid, but I do know one thing. At least I'm sensible. You do what you want, but I'm not going to risk everything."

"You speak as if there's no good reason to risk everything. I don't know why I was given this gift . . ." Red paused, her voice trembling. "But I'm not allowing fear to get in the way of what's important. Do you remember the poem? 'The light that shines in all our lives will save us from a thousand cries'? Trust this, if not me, Will."

Will sighed. "I'll trust the poem because I trust you."

They climbed the staircase in silence. Each feared the burden they now held. Trust was something they desperately needed. But now more than ever, they were glad to have each other.

Chapter
Nine

It was a very quiet night. The faint cry of a bird or a whistle from a tree could sometimes be heard outside. No one could sleep. Red had asked Eleanor when they would leave. Her aunt's only reply was quick and sharp.

"We're not leaving anytime soon. There's no point in going if you haven't mastered your gift yet."

"But you have," Red said.

"Crivvens! What gave you that impression? I'm still learning every day. I fear we would be risking too much for nothing if we went now. You need to learn as much as you can. He has spoken before of a plan to be pursued during winter.

"Of course, years ago, his gift was taken away before winter. But he's had many years to come up with new plans, unfortunately." Eleanor sounded slightly irritated. "But if he does plan to attack during winter, we must be ready. Snow is a more dangerous tool than you think."

"Avalanches are dangerous, though we're far from any chance of that—"

"Red, I don't mean avalanches, though he could make that happen if he wanted to. I've seen a lot of his infamous power, which could very well have grown. You need to trust my words, Red. I have much more experience dealing with him."

"I do trust you, but why can't we defeat him the way you and Arthur did?"

"We didn't defeat him, Red. We just contained him. That's different. It could take months to even find him."

"Well, it's a good thing I'm not going anywhere." Red smiled. Then her smile slowly faded. "How long will all of this take—I mean, finding Callum *and* defeating him?"

"I don't know, Red. I'm not really sure of anything right now."

"I understand," said Red quietly, though she wasn't sure if she actually did.

—⚋—

Red woke up to a rainstorm outside. The rain poured down her window, so she could barely see outside. Claire was still asleep; it was four in the morning.

Red quietly got up. She gave up trying to go back to sleep. She slowly went down the stairs and then stopped when she heard something.

"I see what you mean, but I said no," said a woman's voice from downstairs.

Red hid behind the railing. She peered down the steps and saw Eleanor and two other people talking. Both wore very elaborate outfits. Red couldn't even see the woman's face under her large hat.

"It was not anyone's fault! I understand your concern, but we will take care of it," said Eleanor.

"Some of the other countries are getting scared, and you say a child will save us? You better get her ready before winter, or there will be consequences, Eleanor," said the woman.

Eleanor placed her hands on her head. "That's too little time."

"That is not our problem," said the man. "With Arthur out of the picture, these people rely on *you* to save them. You know most about Callum, so why can't you figure out anything?"

"You think this is easy for me?" Eleanor said sharply. "I want to help her control her power, but I fear it. Her power's a lot stronger than I thought. I'm afraid she'll turn into the same thing he has become. I messed up once. I don't want to risk everything again."

"You know most about him. Don't you have a plan?" asked the woman.

"I *did* know most about him," whispered Eleanor, "but that was a long time ago. He's not the same person I once knew."

Red gasped from behind the railing. She quickly covered her mouth with her hands.

"You have until winter, Eleanor," said the woman.

Then both of them headed out the door. Red could hear the loud clinking of the woman's heels as she walked. The loud slam of the door could've woken everyone up. Eleanor sat down in her chair and stared at the painting of the two young kids. Red had passed by that painting a few times, and every time, she felt a shiver go down her spine. So she avoided it as much as possible.

"Come down here, Red," said Eleanor. She didn't even turn or move her head.

Red poked her head out. "How did you know I was hiding here?"

"I could hear you. We will need to work on that, dear."

Red started down the steps.

"Sit here. We need to talk," said Eleanor.

Red sat down in the chair next to her aunt.

"I need to start preparing you, Red. We have until winter. That's two months to prepare."

Red didn't dare ask what Eleanor meant when she said she knew Callum. She just listened and nodded, though thoughts of worry invaded her mind.

"You ready for that bow and arrows?" asked Eleanor.

She took Red outside, behind the large mansion. Red gasped at what she saw. A large waterfall and many miles of grassland became visible. There were many different kinds of flowers and animals like deer and rabbits.

"How is this possible? We would have seen this when we arrived," said Red, still in awe.

"Like I said to William, you still don't know the definition of *possible* yet, Red." Eleanor took out something she had behind her back. "Also, this is for you."

She held out a beautiful longbow. It had a carving of an oak tree on it. There were also matching arrows.

"This is amazing. Did you make this?" Red took the bow in her hands. It felt empowering.

"Not exactly. It was made by Mr. Stone." Eleanor smiled. "He used to make bows and arrows. Then one day he told me to give this particular one to someone I knew it belonged to. I knew it was you the moment you helped that injured cat when you were four."

Red suddenly remembered that moment. She and her siblings had visited Eleanor when they turned four. Red had heard a strange cry from what she guessed was the garden since she couldn't find the memory too well in her brain. It was a small frail cat with torn hair and was covered in blood. Red had given the cat a bath and treated his wounds. Afterward, she had never seen him again.

"Mr. Stone made this?" asked Red.

"Yes, though that was over many decades ago, before I met Arthur."

"Where is Arthur now?" asked Red without thinking. She noticed that as soon as she asked the question, Eleanor went pale.

"I don't know, dear. A lot of people have been searching for him for the last thirty years. I don't even know if he's alive."

Red was quiet. "You'll find him one day."

Eleanor smiled and nodded hesitantly. "I set up a target near that tree." She pointed to a tree ten meters away. "Let's see what you can do."

"I've never used one before," said Red. "This might take a while."

"I'm gifted, and it took me nearly two decades to be okay at archery. So don't get discouraged."

The sunlight shone across the bow, and a glittering wave of wonder surrounded Red. She took it all in—the simple breeze, the swaying trees, and the quiet hum of Eleanor, who was humming a soft Gaelic tune.

Red took an arrow. She positioned the bow correctly, according to Eleanor's instructions, and fired toward the target. It felt like slow motion to Red, like time was contemplating between two decisions. Finally, the arrow struck. It hit the target, a few inches to the right of the bull's-eye. She rubbed her sore arm and looked toward Eleanor, who smiled under the rays of the sun.

"*Soilleir d' inntinn*. Clear your mind, *mo ghràdh*," she said calmly.

Red breathed in deeply. She closed her eyes and pulled the string back as far as she could pull it. Then she let go. What once was slow and full of questions became fast and full of relief and hopefulness. It was a perfect bull's-eye.

Red smiled as she exhaled. Eleanor laughed with pride as her niece gave her a long hug.

They stayed outside for hours. Eleanor kept moving the target farther until it was over fifty yards away. Red never missed. She felt like the bow was part of her hand.

"You're a natural." Eleanor smiled.

Red tried flexing her arm. "It's sore," she said.

"Don't worry, dear. You'll get used to it." Eleanor smiled.

—◊◊◊—

The sun was nearly setting. Claire, Will, and Bailey sat outside, watching Red shoot the bow. Bailey was in her bear form, so Claire and Will sat a fair distance away from her.

"Do you *have* to be a bear right now?" asked Will.

"I find it amusing," said Bailey.

"Hold on. If you can talk as a bear, why didn't you talk to us when you were leading us out of the woods?" asked Claire.

"It is against the rules. I cannot speak in this form near human towns. Apparently, it isn't normal for animals to talk," said Bailey.

Claire just nodded; she wasn't really sure how to respond.

"Good job, Red. That's another bull's-eye!" said Eleanor. "You caught on a lot faster than I did, though I never really was a bow-and-arrow person."

—◊—

Eleanor decided to make a feast for the children. They all laughed and told stories. Red kept trying to get Eleanor to talk about herself and Arthur.

After almost twenty hints from Red, Eleanor gave in. "Well, alright then. We were in the middle of a battle between the gifted and very few humans against Callum and his army. Arthur and I were tired, though we knew we had to do something quick. Then out of the blue, Arthur walked up to Callum and made some big speech."

"Arthur's request," said Red, smiling.

"Yep. Though it was meaningful, I never really understood it at the time. I do now. We didn't defeat him, Red, even though we tried many times. I hope you can." Eleanor's smile deepened. "I know that's asking a lot, especially since you're only thirteen, but I see a lot more in you than you might see in yourself. Questions like 'Why does the sun rise in the morning and set in the evening?' can throw you off course even if you don't understand why, but remember, you do not need to question everything in life, dear. Just find peace in the answers given to you. We were chosen to hold this gift, and we have the choice to use it for good or evil. Which do you choose, Red?"

Red looked up at Eleanor. "The light that shines in all our lives will save us from a thousand cries."

"Very good, dear. Very good."

—m—

The next morning, Eleanor decided to start helping Red with her gift. They were in the garden behind the mansion. Nobody wanted to go near the rotten one.

"Alright, now sit down," said Eleanor. "Hold this." She gave Red a flower that had not bloomed yet.

"What shall I do with it?" asked Red, who carefully traced a crease in the flower with her finger.

"Well, you help it grow. Share your positive feelings with it. Give it a path to feel welcomed."

Red closed her eyes and cupped her hands. She opened her eyes. "Did it work?"

"Red, you need to feel the flower. Feel your emotions fill the flower with potential. Just like a river that flows, let your feelings flow in the same way and give it life and spirit."

"That seems like a lot of spirit for one flower," said Red.

"Why do you doubt, Red?" asked Eleanor gently. "A flower today can mean the world tomorrow. Have faith in its petals and beauty, and give *it* faith. Do you have faith, Red?"

"Yes, Aunt Eleanor," said Red. She closed her eyes again and tried to feel her feelings. It seemed a tad counterintuitive, but Red didn't question it.

It was hard to feel when simply told to feel. Red could feel beads of sweat forming on her forehead, but she reminded herself that this was Eleanor, who wouldn't get mad if this didn't work.

Was it the way the trees swayed in the cool autumn wind that calmed her down? Or was it the protection she felt having her aunt watch her attempt this so-called impossible feat? She soon felt happiness and light. She felt the warmth of the sun.

Then she opened her eyes.

The bud in her hands had become a beautiful golden flower.

"See what happens when you have faith?" said Eleanor, grinning proudly. "This is your gift, Red. Use it wisely."

They headed back toward the house. Bailey was in her bear form, chasing Will around, and Claire was reading near the fireplace.

"So how did it go?" asked Claire. She wasn't bothered by Will's screams.

"It went great. I feel great," said Red, smiling.

"I'm glad. It's nice seeing you smile. I thought you would destroy the mansion or something like that," said Claire.

"Thank you." Red laughed.

"Red, can you help me out here?" yelled Will.

"No, this is kind of entertaining."

—∿—

By evening, Bailey finally stopped tormenting Will.

"You know, if I was gifted, I could outrun you," said Will.

"You do realize it has nothing to do with that, right? You get tired after walking up the stairs." Claire laughed.

Red and Eleanor nodded simultaneously.

"Red is doing very good with her training," said Eleanor. "We should be done before winter."

"That sounds great. Do you have any ideas on how to defeat him yet?" asked Red.

Eleanor shook her head. "Not yet, I'm afraid. I've never seen his power this strong before. It's a bit odd."

"Aunt Eleanor, I have a question," asked Red.

"Yes, dear?"

"Well, when I overheard you talking to those people, you said something about how you used to know Callum."

Eleanor paused. "I did say that." She sighed.

There was a slight shift in the room. It felt unmistakably drafty, even though all the windows were shut. Red felt an awkward sensation climb the back of her neck and rest on her shoulder, waiting. Eleanor retreated to her armchair, which was walnut brown and torn at the sides. She lifted her tea cup to her lips and seemed entranced by the flames in her fireplace.

"We were like you three once—Arthur, Callum, and I. Arthur and I weren't able to save Callum. I consider that my own mistake."

"You're not responsible for his actions," said Red. "I just don't understand how such a great gift can turn a person evil."

Eleanor shook her head. "It's not the gift, dear. It's what the person decides to do with the gift that can turn them evil. One day, they just turn into someone you don't recognize anymore."

"That sounds awful," said Red quietly.

Eleanor nodded. "Even the purest of hearts can become blinded. But many can still shine through the darkness—that's the beauty of our gift."

There was an unexpected knock on the front door.

Eleanor walked over to the door. She first checked through the windows to see who it was. It was a tall man apparently delivering a letter. He left the letter on the porch and then quickly left.

Eleanor opened the door. "Post doesn't usually come at this hour."

"What does the letter say?" asked Claire.

Eleanor took a moment to read the letter, and her eyes grew wide. She cleared her throat. "There is a little change of plans," she said almost apprehensively. "We're all needed at a private meeting. It's a two-day walk, so get water and food."

"Meeting? What meeting?" asked Will.

"You know those two people I was talking to before?" Eleanor asked Red. "They're basically the mayors of this area. They want all of us to come for a meeting. I don't have a clue why."

"When do we leave?" asked Red. The idea of leaving so soon bothered her.

"As soon as we can," said Eleanor. "We can stay at Mr. Stone's inn."

Red noticed Bailey cringe when Eleanor talked about being in the woods after dark. Red suspected she had had a few encounters with creatures other than that other bear they had seen before. Eleanor grabbed a small bag and packed some canteens of water and some food.

"Stay close, children. You don't want to get lost in this wood.

Chapter

Ten

Red looked up at the sky as she walked with the others. She had many doubts and worries.

Faith and trust—that's all you really need, she thought.

Eleanor had asked Bailey to walk in her bear form in order to scare off any predators or people for that matter. None of them were in the mood for any socializing at the moment. Luckily, they were far from any human towns.

"You said this was a two-day walk?" asked Will.

Eleanor nodded. "You'll survive, William. Just keep up. There are a lot of unfriendly creatures in these woods."

The path was covered in leaves, and whistling wind fluttered past their ears. Earlier, Eleanor had told Red many stories of thriving countries so beautiful that one could only suspect magic to be their only source. One special country known as the Gifted Land Country was Red's favourite.

"This is not some wild myth or tale, dear," Eleanor had said while she told the stories, "but true wonders even I still haven't been able to comprehend."

—◊◊—

A few hours had passed. The group was sick of the endless trees and still nothing new in view. It was nearly noon. The trees covered most of their view of the sky, so it was hard to tell. Will constantly asked when they would take a break, and Eleanor would always say, "We cannot be out here at night, William."

It was blunt, but Red understood. Eleanor had also told her stories of creatures that came out at night. Not so much foxes and frogs but creatures known as night corpses.

Eleanor had thoroughly explained what they were. "Vicious and untrustworthy, they can transform their appearance into anything— an object or a person. They feel nothing. Their true origin is hard to determine, but some say they were once gifted individuals who used their power for evil. And now they have teamed up with Callum."

Red wanted to know more about the countries, so she quietly tapped Eleanor on the shoulder. "Would you tell me more about the countries?"

Eleanor smiled. She was glad Red was interested. "*Tha*, well, everything in this world is known as the Gifted Lands, but the main country is also called the Gifted Land Country, the original. It took its first breath many blue moons ago. It's located in the center of all the countries. One country, Elle, means 'snow.' It's located far north and is home to many people. The next country, Wildur, was named after my old friend Arthur Wildur. It is near the east. It is a wooded area, and the only language they speak is English. The people there are very sociable and sweet."

"Well, that's nice," said Red. "I would love to visit Wildur."

Eleanor continued, "Another country is Elivar, which translates to 'wise.' It is in the south, and its people are known as the Ará, or 'shape-shifter.' This is the country where Bailey is from."

"It used to be a wonderful place," said Bailey quietly. "But since Callum got to it, it's never been the same. Everyone who used to be full of wisdom are now relying on fear and doubt. I fear it will stay that way forever."

"I don't believe that," said Red. "Evil never wins."

Eleanor silently smiled. "Very good, dear."

"What about the other country you mentioned?" asked Red.

"Oh yes," said Eleanor reluctantly, "*Tir na h-Oidhche*, in Gaelic, translates to 'night land.' It's also called the Land of Night. We're not really sure about this area. All we know is, that's where Callum decided to stay. It was part of Elivar a long time ago, but it became its own country, Nóctewl, which is 'night' in Irish, roughly five centuries ago. Now, Callum has turned it into a country of careless destruction."

"Did Mr. Stone do anything about it?" asked Red.

"He can't do anything about that."

"But I thought you said he was more powerful than anyone in this world."

"Everything happens for a reason, mo ghràdh," she said with a quiet smile.

"There is also a small country in between Elle and the Land of Night called Tìr an Uisge, which means Land of Water in Gaelic. The people can actually breathe underwater. Though it is also home to many sea monsters, who usually eat people."

"That sounds scary," said Will.

Eleanor smiled. "It is not to be confused with the Gifted Sea, which surrounds everything."

"How is this even possible?" asked Claire, who finally said something after pondering everything Eleanor had said. "How have we not heard of any of this? And why are some countries in Gaelic?"

"That worries me, Claire," said Eleanor. "You lack faith in what I am telling you. You need faith in order to see the many countries." Eleanor had a ruminative expression, which soon lightened. "And to answer your other question, some countries have their own languages like in your world, but most speak either English, Gaelic, or the gifted speech."

Red thought about what Eleanor said. "How does that work, like about needing faith to see the countries?"

"Having faith means believing even without any evidence, which happens to be what this world is built on."

"That seems hard," said Will.

"Yes, it is. But my parents have always told me, '*Tha misteach nas gaisge na gaisgeachd*.' Courage is braver than bravery."

Red noticed that the trees surrounding them had a soft golden twinkle, like some sort of dreamlike hallucination. It was beautiful. She walked over to one without realizing it, and she placed a hand on a branch without reason, just wonder.

And a wonder it was!

The branches started growing an extraordinary dark brown, and gold leaves sprang from the branches, creating an array of picturesque wonder around the young girl.

The others noticed and walked over. Though it was hard to tell considering she was in her bear form, Bailey, too, was enjoying the delightful sight.

"I could never get used to this," said Red, still in awe.

"I still haven't." Eleanor smiled, gently placing a hand on Red's shoulder.

—⟶—

It was starting to get late. Red had feared this would happen. The others looked at Eleanor for guidance. She tried to keep a calm façade, though she, too, was starting to get worried.

"Mr. Stone's Inn is just around the corner," Eleanor said. "But do be mindful. This inn is very old, so try not to break anything." She eyed Red and Will.

After around fifteen minutes, they reached a rather small cottage. It was charming, Red noticed. The cottage's door was tenuous in some ways, though beautifully crafted. There was a large oak tree symbol on it. Red wondered why that symbol was everywhere she looked.

"Go on. Give it a knock," said Will, who at the moment was hiding behind Eleanor.

Red walked over to the door. Though she felt a bit hesitant for some reason, she still proceeded to knock. She knocked twice. For a minute or two, there was nothing, no sound. Then the door opened. A tall old man with a beard opened the door. He wore a brown coat with the oak tree symbol on it as well.

"Mr. Stone," said Eleanor with a smile, "lovely to see you again."

"Likewise, Eleanor," said Mr. Stone. "And whom have you brought here?"

"These are my nieces and nephew—Red, Claire, and Will. And this is Bailey."

Mr. Stone eyed Red. "You are a gifted. I can see it in your eyes."

Red looked at Eleanor, and she wondered how Mr. Stone knew so quickly. She looked around the room. It was a lot bigger on the inside, which was odd, but Red didn't question it. There were many carpets and picture frames, all with oak tree markings engraved on its borders.

"Good thing you all got here before nightfall. That wouldn't have been pretty," Mr. Stone said. "I got word that a pack of Callum's wolves were hunting around these areas—looking for people to eat or use as spies, I wouldn't doubt. We're a great distance from Tir na h-Oidhche, so the prisoners will probably be dead before the wolves can get to *Callum.*"

This didn't help Will at all. He trembled and probably was now realizing just what he was getting into.

"No need to fear, lad," said Mr. Stone gently. "You got a great family here who will protect you, and you shall protect them in turn."

Will shook his head. "I'm no warrior or protector. I'm a coward."

Mr. Stone placed a hand on Will's shoulder. "What I see is a young man who is a lot braver than he chooses to believe." He then looked at Bailey. "I see a strong and wise protector." He looked to Claire. "I see a young woman who is loyal and intelligent beyond her years." He then turned to Red. "I see a courageous heart who will defeat Callum and restore our Gifted Lands."

Their group was silent, but Eleanor smiled. She had known Mr. Stone since she was a young girl. He was always giving good advice. Sometimes she understood. Now that she has grown older and wiser, she felt very grateful.

"Listen to his words, children," said Eleanor. "I wouldn't be here today if I haven't listened."

The group shared a glance.

"What do you mean?" asked Red.

"That's a story for another time, mo ghràdh. It's getting pretty late."

Mr. Stone walked over to a tiny closet past a large fireplace. Inside was a pile of blankets for them.

"Yes, I have these here if you want them." He passed out the blankets. "I haven't had any visitors in over a decade, believe it or not." He scratched his head. "Well, that means the entire second floor is yours for however long you need."

"Thank you," the company said gratefully.

The rooms were cozy. They reminded Red of the rooms Eleanor had at her mansion, though these rooms were like cottage living rooms. Each had a small fireplace.

It's wonderful, she thought. Then she wondered why no one wanted to stay here.

Will was afraid of bugs, so he decided to stand on his bed until Eleanor yelled at him. Claire found a small library and started reading, while Bailey stared off into the woods from a window.

"What's the matter?" asked Claire.

"You never know," answered Bailey. "Mr. Stone said there was a pack of wolves running around here. I'm just taking extra precautions."

"That's not needed, dear," said Mr. Stone. "Even if there were a few wolves here, they don't have any way of getting in." He turned to Red. "And I'm sure she knows how to handle a bow if anything ever happens."

Red smiled sheepishly. "Hopefully."

———✀———

That night, the winds were strong. Mr. Stone had mentioned earlier that there was going to be a storm. Red wondered how he knew that so soon. The storm was loud and frightening. She wondered how Will was dealing with it. She got up, groaning. Her back and legs ached from walking. She trudged over to Will's room and knocked.

Will answered it. His eyes were red, and there were dark bags under his eyes.

"I'm sorry. Did I wake you?" asked Red.

Red noticed Will was clutching a brown stuffed bear. Once he noticed her glance at it, he quickly hid it behind his back.

"No. No. You didn't wake me. I was just uh . . ."

"The stuffed bear I gave you on our seventh birthday," said Red with a smile, "you still keep it."

"I can't sleep without it. Just a habit, I guess," said Will, his cheeks bright red.

Then out of the blue, there was a swift knock on the door downstairs. Red and Will became deathly silent. They really had to reason to be.

Wolves can't knock, thought Red.

Mr. Stone and Eleanor apparently also heard the knocking, and each came out of their rooms, which were across from each other, almost at the same time.

"Who would be outside at this hour?" grumbled Mr. Stone. He quickly walked downstairs and slowly peered through the window next to the door. He glanced at Eleanor.

"What in the world?" he said. He stumbled as he tried to open the door quickly.

There, out in the stormy, rainy night was a young boy around six years old. Eleanor gasped and quickly led the child inside from the pouring rain.

Will eyed the child suspiciously.

Chapter

Eleven

The sky was dark and ominous. Red ran over to grab a few blankets for the young boy. Eleanor and Mr. Stone tried talking to him, but at the moment, the child appeared to be too scared to talk.

Will kept a fair distance from the child. He wouldn't even look at him. Claire and Bailey were still asleep. Red had noticed that both of them were heavy sleepers. She was a bit glad that Bailey was upstairs. She wondered if her friend would scare the child even more by interrogating him.

"He doesn't want to talk," said Eleanor, finally standing up. She, too, had dark circles under her eyes and looked as though she hadn't slept a wink for weeks.

"Could I try talking to him?" asked Red, who was a bit surprised at her sudden trust.

She walked over slowly to the young boy and then took a seat next to him. The others left the room.

"Hello," said Red.

The young boy still glanced away. Red noticed that he had large brown eyes and scruffy brown hair.

"My name is Red," she said. "Do you have a name?"

"Max," squeaked the young boy.

Red smiled. At least she got his name.

"Where do you live, Max?"

For a couple of minutes, the young boy was silent. Then a few more minutes passed. Red wondered how she would find out where he lived.

"Is it cold where you live?" asked Red.

The boy shook his head.

Then Red thought of another question. "So how do you feel about trees?" She cringed at her question.

The boy shook his head.

Red's shoulders slumped. She knew she was close, or at least she thought she was.

"Do you like water?" she asked, too tired to understand what a vague question she had asked.

The young boy nodded his head slowly.

Red smiled. "Can you shapeshift?"

Max shook his head.

Mr. Stone and Eleanor walked in. Eleanor was carrying many more blankets, which were stacked so high her face couldn't be seen. Red stood up and walked over to them. She noticed the boy glance toward the window with a look of awe on his face like he'd never seen trees before in his life.

"What have you found?" asked Mr. Stone.

"Well, his name is Maxwell, and I believe he's from Tìr an Uisge," said Red with little confidence.

"Tìr an Uisge?" echoed Mr. Stone. "That's hundreds of miles northwest from here. How in the world did he get here?"

They peered into the room, where Max sat. Will walked over to them. He was still skeptical about this child's story.

"I heard the questions you were asking him, Red. Even if he likes water, it doesn't mean he's from Tìr an Uisge," said Will.

"Will, he said he couldn't shapeshift, so he's not from Elivar. There are no forests where he lives, so he's not from Wildur. Plus, he was staring at the trees from the window like he'd never seen them before. It isn't cold where he lives, so he isn't from Elle."

"Did you ask him if he was from the Gifted Lands or Tìr na h-Oidhche?"

Red shook her head. "I didn't think of that."

"Let's hope he's from neither of those places," stated Eleanor. "He doesn't look like he can handle the abilities of a gifted at his age. But a lot of families are taking ships away from the Land of Night. I wonder if he got separated from his parents."

"He's not a gifted, Eleanor," said Mr. Stone. "He doesn't have that twinkle in his eye. But I don't know how we can even get him back to his family. That could take months. And I don't want to take a child hundreds of miles only to find out he doesn't actually live there. We don't know much about him. We shouldn't act until we find more information."

"That sounds fair," said Red calmly. "But what are we going to do now?"

"He'll have to stay in a room," said Eleanor.

She walked over to Max and asked him if he wanted to rest in a room. The young boy nodded and stood up.

"Thank you," he said. His voice was high-pitched and shaky.

"You're very welcome," said Mr. Stone. "Now head upstairs. You can take the first room on the right."

"I am still against this," whispered Will. "We just let a possibly dangerous stranger into the cottage where we are. Who knows what could happen?"

"No, William. We let in a soaking wet child who is terrified and doesn't have anywhere else to go," said Mr. Stone gently. "I know you don't agree with this, but we need to help the child. This is the worst storm I've seen in decades. And who knows what lurks outside? Many creatures would be thriving in this kind of weather."

"But we didn't see any clouds outside before we came here," said Will.

"Well, I suppose it's a bit hard to see the sky with all the trees," said Red.

Will turned toward her. "This is all your fault," he snarled.

"My fault?" Red almost laughed. "I'm not the cause of *every* rainstorm, William."

"Children, please," started Eleanor. "There is no need to fuss over this. Red, dear, it's not your fault. The weather has been acting up for a while now."

"You might be here for a while. I don't know how long this storm will last. You could be here for weeks," said Mr. Stone.

"Weeks?" said Will with a squeak. "Storms don't last weeks."

"This area shares roughly the same weather patterns as Wildur. It rarely rains there, but every so often, when it does, it lasts for a couple of weeks."

Red and Will sighed. This journey was getting a lot more complicated.

"Looks like we're going to miss that meeting," said Eleanor. "I had completely forgotten until now." She turned to Will. "Hand me a piece of parchment, William. Thank you."

Eleanor started writing in a language Red didn't understand. The letters were beautiful and neatly written. They reminded Red of a swirling waterfall that glides across the paper with ease.

"What language are you writing in?" she asked as she watched her aunt write effortlessly.

"Gifted speech, mo ghràdh."

"I want to learn gifted speech," said Red, fascinated.

"Well, it won't be hard for you to catch on. You have gifted blood running in your veins."

Red looked up at her aunt in surprise. "Really?" she said quietly. "I guess I haven't thought of that until now." She then looked up at her aunt. "Then why aren't Claire and Will gifted?"

"It's like a recessive gene. Not everyone in the family will get it." Eleanor placed a hand on her niece's shoulder. "I promise you will see the Gifted Land, mo ghràdh." She smiled. "No matter what."

—⁂—

The next morning was freezing, even with the fireplace. Red, Eleanor, Mr. Stone, and Will didn't sleep that much last night. None of them really felt suspicious of young Max except Will.

After a couple of days, his suspicion grew. On the other hand, Bailey and Claire only felt pity for the young child once they met him.

"I don't understand," said Will. He was outside with Red, underneath a wooden canopy, helping Mr. Stone with his gardening.

"What don't you get?" asked Mr. Stone. He handed Red some small brown seeds and then gestured toward an empty flowerbed.

"Max. How did he get here in the first place?" Will continued. "We're missing something."

Red started placing the small seeds into the warm soil. She looked at her brother and then at Mr. Stone. A look of reluctance surfaced on her face.

"I hate to admit it, but I'm starting to agree with him," she said without making eye contact with Mr. Stone.

Mr. Stone scratched his head. "I've had that same feeling, children. Though I am not yet sure, we still need to show kindness."

"But what if we're wrong, and he's some sort of creature out to get us?" said Will.

"There's a reason for everything, William," said Mr. Stone deliberately. "I don't want you to act out or do anything to the young chap. Whatever happens, you will find your way back again."

Will eyed Red, who also seemed confused.

"What do you mean 'find your way back again'?" she asked.

"All I'm going to tell you is that there are many people you can trust. Be smart about that."

That was all that was said for the day. But thoughts and questions and rumors invaded Red and Will's minds as they slept through the cold night.

—⚬—

Nearly a week after the group found shelter at the old inn, the rain was finally clearing up, and Eleanor was cleaning nonstop.

Young Max started speaking a lot more, but he was still a bit shy when the question was about where he lived. There was much talk of the different countries, though Max didn't seem to know anything about them. The group had really warmed up to the child, even Will, who started to have a conversation with him. It went like this.

"Do you miss your family?" Will asked.

The young boy looked up toward the trees through the window. "Yes. Do you?"

Will thought about his parents. "Very much. But now we have this task we need to do, and I'm not sure how to do it yet," sighed Will.

"Task?" Max asked curiously.

"Yes." Will hesitated at first, but the young child's curious eyes were very reassuring. "We need to defeat *Callum*, but we don't know where to start."

"Who's he?"

"He's this evil gifted man who went crazy, I guess," said Will. His description was vague yet accurate. "But there's a lot we need to do before we even have a chance of defeating him."

"I'm sure you all can do it. Your sister seems pretty good with a bow."

Will laughed. "Yes, I guess she is. But we're going to need a lot more than that."

"I'm scared," said Max. "What if I never see my family again?"

"You will," said Will. "I promise."

Max turned toward the window. "So what will you all do now?"

Will looked out toward the window as well. He now understood why Red always looked out windows. The view of the trees were relaxing and comforting.

"Aunt Eleanor said something about getting help from people in Wildur. So that means many more miles of walking, unfortunately."

"You should also get help from Elle. Their army is very large, and they will be more than willing to help you out," said Max. His eyes were calm and wise. His voice was as serene as his words.

Will nodded in agreement. "I should let the others know."

"Yes, you should," said the young boy.

—⁓—

"Elle? Helpful?" cried Mr. Stone. "Elle hasn't been helpful in over five hundred years!"

"Well, it had made sense then," said Will, who was now strangely reluctant about going. "What do you think, Aunt Eleanor?"

Eleanor shook her head. "Sorry, William, but Mr. Stone is right. I wouldn't trust Elle with anything."

Mr. Stone eyed the young child from the other room. He closed his eyes and sighed. Then he stood up and led everyone upstairs.

"You all listen to me right now," said Mr. Stone sternly. "If you want to get out of here alive, then don't make eye contact with it, and keep walking out the door downstairs. Am I clear?"

"It?" asked Eleanor, surprised. "*He* is a young boy who needs our help."

"Eleanor, you need to trust me." Mr. Stone's eyes were unwavering. He turned to Red. "You *all* need to trust me."

"Alright," said Red.

Mr. Stone grab a large box underneath the bed. "Did you bring your bow?"

Red quickly grabbed the majestic bow and her quiver of arrows from her room. "How did you know?"

Mr. Stone opened the box, and inside was a shining silver sword with tree engravings. "Keep that bow safe, and use it only when you have to, which could very well mean right now."

"What?" said Red, shaking her head.

"Hide it behind your back, Red. You"—he turned to Bailey—"guard the front door, just in case anything happens."

The group slowly climbed down the staircase. Red hid her bow behind her back, as she was told. Young Max was sitting silently on the couch.

"Are you all leaving already?" he asked.

"Yes," said Red. "It was nice meeting you, Max, but we need to get going."

"To Elle?"

"Yes," answered Mr. Stone quickly.

"Why are you carrying a sword and she a bow?" asked the child. "And why are you hiding them from me?"

Mr. Stone eyed the child, who stood up and glared at Red. His gaze was deathly and menacing.

"So little time yet so little effort," Max said. "You really think you can defeat him? You think you're special?" He eyed Red. "Do you know what you're risking? Do you understand that what you're doing is pointless?"

"But you were talking to me, and you said you were scared," said Will. "What do you gain from this?"

Max smiled. "Child, I am hundreds of years older than you. You don't know *anything*. You have no idea."

Just then, the young boy's smile became twisted. His teeth became razor sharp, and his skin turned pale. His eyes turned bloodred, and he grew twice in size. That was no little boy.

"Night corpse," whispered Mr. Stone.

Chapter

Twelve

The room was deathly silent. No one wanted to move. Red grabbed an arrow from her quiver, while Mr. Stone made Claire and Will stand behind him. All the fires in the inn went out.

The night corpse had an empty stare and seemed as if he were to jump at any second. Mr. Stone took a few steps toward the nasty creature. He drew his sword, though he kept it beside him.

"We don't want any trouble, but if you move, I will have no problem killing you."

"Perhaps you will."

Mr. Stone gripped his sword tighter. "What do you mean by that?"

Silence.

"Speak!"

The creature smiled again, but this time, it seemed as if he were melting—melting into the same little boy. Mr. Stone glared at him.

"You think that would stop me?" said Mr. Stone. "In your foul mind, you believe nothing can stop evil. Your kind may also be hundreds of years old, but I've seen powers way stronger than you'll ever understand. You'll never win."

The creature laughed, but it seemed less menacing coming from a little boy. Mr. Stone lifted his sword. He looked over to Red.

Red closed her eyes. Something, a feeling, washed over her whole body. She opened her eyes, and a wave of calm and serene wind fluttered past her unwavering eyes. She was ready.

"Why are you here?" asked Mr. Stone. "What's your purpose?"

"I was simply taking orders from my master. And if you assume you can get a word out of me, you're deeply mistaken. For years, we learned and watched the ways of your kind, unseen." The creature smiled, slowly turning into his true form.

At that moment, Red shot the arrow with ease. The creature was so focused on laughing he didn't notice the arrow in his chest. In the next moment, there was no evil in the room anymore.

Eleanor gave her niece a large hug, and the rest of the family joined in.

"Another act of bravery," said Eleanor. "Well done, mo ghràdh, though I'm sorry you had to experience something like this."

"I'll be alright," said Red. "I have you and them." She turned toward her siblings, Bailey, and Mr. Stone.

"Yes, dear. But I'm afraid that won't be the last arrow you will fire," said Mr. Stone. "I've noticed something in you I haven't seen in anyone for a long while. Courage, my dear. Courage."

—⚏—

The group surrounded the living room fire. It was notably quiet other than the singing of Eleanor, who sang "Auld Lang Syne" with so much heart that no one dared to interrupt her.

Red listened to her aunt and watched as the tired-sounding words elegantly glided along her aunt's mouth and onto the warm dry air. It seemed everyone else shared her wonder and enjoyment. When Eleanor stopped, she turned her head toward Mr. Stone, who seemed too entranced by the song to notice. He finally looked up at Eleanor's kind eyes.

"I know," he said and proceeded to follow the smoke from the fire with his eyes.

"Tomorrow morning, right when the sun peeks its head beyond the mountain, you all shall leave for Elivar. I will let Lady Ava know of your arrival. The Ará are not fond of unknown visitors."

"What are you talking about?" asked Red.

"Tomorrow, we will continue our way to the land of Elivar only because of its closeness. But I am not that happy about it," said Eleanor.

"Why not?" asked Will.

"A while ago, I did something to make their queen, Lady Ava, angry. I haven't seen her since then, and I fear she still holds a grudge."

"It'll be alright, Aunt Eleanor," said Red. "I'm sure she's nothing to be afraid of."

Mr. Stone and Eleanor shared a quick glance. Eleanor took a long sip of tea. The other four could only imagine what she was thinking.

—∿—

Morning came.

The moss on the tall lengthy trees glistened golden. Red watched it for many minutes. The scenery was a gift in the early hours of the morning, and if you were lucky, you would be able to share in its beauty.

"Alright, let's head off," said Eleanor. She looked at Mr. Stone with no words but with a smile that said everything.

"Will we ever see you again?" Red asked Mr. Stone.

"Of course, when the time is right."

She wondered what that meant, but she ultimately decided not to question it.

For a while after they left the inn, they simply walked without any conversation. No one really felt the need to speak, especially since Eleanor was usually the first to start a conversation. But this time, it was Red who broke the silence.

"Tell us more about Elivar, Aunt Eleanor," she said.

Eleanor was quiet for a few moments. "Well, it's a wonderful place. The Ará are very conservative, though, and don't like interactions that much. The rest of the Gifted Lands aren't very fond of Elivar right now. The Ará quickly restored their land after Callum destroyed it, and everyone has since asked them for help in defeating him. But Lady Ava and the Ará refused, not wanting to risk the safety of their people."

The children stayed silent, not knowing how to respond. Or it was because of the blinding sun flooding through their eyelids.

They had walked for a while, enough where the sun danced across the sky to meet the trees in the west. Red found it conspicuously amazing—nature. This place was a lot more green than back home in London, and it was a lot drier too. It seemed her siblings shared her thoughts, as their eyes also shifted from tree to tree.

Bailey walked in her bear form; she had said it was easier that way to walk long distances.

Suddenly, Eleanor stopped dead in her tracks. Her head turned with slight discomfort.

There in front of her were gilded gates with flowering vines woven into them. They tried to look away, but to no avail. The sun's shining teeth glittered wildly along the gate's brilliant picture, which shone a million stars above them.

Finally, they were able to walk beyond the gate.

It was beautiful.

Mountains with towns beyond the cool autumn gaze. Not enough flowers could ever complete its scenery.

"It's glorious," said Red.

Eleanor watched the land with a half-smile. Red glanced at her quizzically. Eleanor smoothed the wrinkles on her dress and her crown of flowers with some tranquil emotion.

"You seem less than amazed, Aunt Eleanor," said Red. "Even after a million visits, this would never get old."

"It is very lovely," said her aunt, "but nothing can compare to the beauty of the Gifted Land Country." She closed her eyes. "Close your eyes, mo ghràdh. Feel the cold wind fly across your tired eyes. Imagine pillars of white and gold so tall that they seem like they can steal the stars right out of the sky. The nights are not nearly as dark there, for the country is illuminated by joy and courage."

Red saw it.

At first, she was confused about where she was. But she could hear her aunt's voice through the leaves on the trees.

Trees were spread across mountains of green. It was like a dream. Red wasn't asleep, though. As odd as it was, she felt completely content. She continued to feel the starlit wind, wherever it came from. It was a feeling she had never felt before.

She opened her eyes. "That was amazing!"

"Yes, it was," said Claire.

The rest of the group had also seen it.

"Follow me," said Eleanor. She paused for a moment and then continued along a trail of flowers.

Soon they entered a small town. Everyone wore outfits that were clean and barely had any wrinkles, though they all shared the same half-smile. Red sheepishly waved, but her gesture wasn't nearly as inconspicuous as she wanted it to be.

"Don't make long eye contact with anybody," said Eleanor. "Heads down."

Then from beyond a small cottage, three soldiers in blue quickly walked toward them and proceeded to push them toward a large castle, much to the group's chagrin.

They entered the brilliant castle. The soldiers led them toward the center of a hall with massive white pillars.

A woman in a long white robe stood before them. Red concluded that this must be Lady Ava, the queen.

She had long brown hair and ice-cold eyes. She said something in a smooth yet loud voice, and it filled the room, giving people the chills.

Red guessed she had spoken in gifted speech.

"Eleanor Watson," Lady Ava said, "Mr. Stone told me of your travels." Her smile slowly changed. "Why are you here?"

Eleanor's shuffled her feet on the marble floor as she chose her words. "Lady Ava," she said, "we had to leave the inn, the reason being our own business. I only ask for civility, not friendship."

Red noticed the soldiers cringe as they turned their heads.

"You shall be blind or a fool to label yourself superior, Watson." The queen's stare was relentless. "You speak of intrinsic civility, and yet you have the audacity to determine our own altruism." She took a few steps forward, and then she turned to Red.

"Who is she?"

Red turned toward her aunt. Eleanor still eyed the queen fearlessly. "She is Red Watson, my niece."

The queen's face suddenly lit up, and she slowly walked toward Red. "Is it true, child? Are you willing to risk everything for the good of others?"

Red nodded.

"Speak, or all is for naught!"

"Yes, I am," said Red, avoiding the queen's ice-cold eyes.

Lady Ava shouted something in her country's tongue, and one of the soldiers proceeded toward her. A young woman around fifteen with wavy black hair and chestnut brown eyes looked up toward the queen.

"Clara, please escort our guests to their living quarters. Thank you, dear."

"Of course, Lady Ava," Clara said. She then turned toward the group company. "Follow me."

They followed the young woman, who shared no conversation with them. Red noticed that Will was as red as a tomato and was staring at the floor as he walked.

"Just in there," said Clara. "You all will have your own rooms."

The soldier pointed toward a wonderfully cozy living area, with separate rooms for each of them.

"If you need anything, please ask," Clara said in a bittersweet tone. "Lady Ava is very busy and will not except interruptions of any kind."

They all nodded, still entranced by the great walls of stone and the tall ceilings of white and gray.

"Thank you," said Will.

Clara nodded and quickly walked out of the room. Eleanor finally turned to Bailey, who had returned to her human form when they had reached the gate.

"How does it feel to be home?" Eleanor asked.

Bailey smiled, gripping her necklace in her palm. "I feel like the world is staring to make sense again," she said, looking at the Watson children as well, "especially because of you four."

Eleanor took a moment to regroup. She couldn't help but feel proud of the children. They all went to bed contentedly, but Eleanor couldn't sleep.

She wondered why the Ará were so welcoming. She believed it had something to do with Red. She soon succumbed to rationality and fell asleep.

—⏳—

The next day, Eleanor told them to explore. Though with two raised eyebrows and a long exhale, she trusted in the fact that these children were more than capable of defending themselves.

As they were leaving, however, she looked at them with uncertainty. "*Fuirich sàbhailte*, stay safe."

When Eleanor was left alone in the room, her stomach flowed onto the marble flooring.

Red was accompanied by Claire. They were going to explore the country's stables, much to Claire's annoyance. It smelled musty and stale. On one wall were hay bales that were stacked to the ceiling, and the aroma of horse breath was rather uncomfortable.

The stables were beautiful, and each stall had the oak tree symbol carved into it.

"Interesting," said Red under her breath.

Claire realized that she had stepped on something squishy and dared not to look under her boot.

"I think you mean terrible," she said.

Red laughed quietly. Suddenly, she heard something in the near distance away from the stables. She didn't know whether to feel disturbed or scared by it. It sounded like a hurt animal.

A hand was placed onto Red's shoulder, and she quickly turned round to find Lady Ava looking down at her.

"Quite jumpy today, aren't we?"

Red patted down her cardigan to avoid looking directly at the queen's eyes.

"You girls may choose a horse to accompany you on your journey, wherever that may be." The queen gestured to the horses, who all seemed to share the same "avoiding eye contact" preference.

"Thank you," said Red. She finally had to look up at her pale blue eyes. They looked like they were frozen over by a sheet of silver snow. She noticed that Lady Ava was wearing a less-elegant white dress and was missing her crown.

"I don't want dirt all over my robe," said the queen, noticing Red's interest, "and I expect you both to follow my directions and to not go off somewhere." Her words were blunt and quick, and Red suspected they were specifically directed toward her.

And with that Lady Ava left, leaving two confused yet intrigued girls.

"Isn't this amazing?" asked Red, continuing to walk toward a white and brown horse.

Claire scrunched her nose. "I don't know," she said, taking a few steps away from a horse. "I don't know if we should trust them."

"Of course, we can trust them! I can see it in their eyes." Red started petting an all-black horse, who neighed with delight.

Claire let out an exasperated sigh and kicked some hay out of the way so she could walk closer to her sister.

"I mean theArá folk!" she whispered harshly.

Red looked down as she pet the horse, saying nothing.

Then she heard it again.

She couldn't quite identify it, though, whatever that sound was. Claire noticed her attention drifting.

"What?"

Red started walking toward the other opening of the stables. As she drew closer, the sound stopped. The silence was deafening without it.

"Stay here," she said, preoccupied. "I'll be right back."

"But Aunt Eleanor told us to stay safe, which includes you," Claire called out. But nobody was there to answer back.

—⁂—

Will and Bailey were invited to check out the village. They were accompanied by Lady Ava. It was almost as beautiful as the first time they were there, though the queen explained the circumstances for that.

"Every year, there's a fest to celebrate the day I saved our land from getting destroyed by the king's treacherous son. In English, the feast is called Divine Flower, which symbolizes the rebirth of our civilization. Every year, a flower is planted in our garden."

Will stopped walking, and as a result, Bailey bumped into him. "What do you mean by 'the king's treacherous son'?"

Lady Ava eyed the boy with confusion. "Hasn't that aunt of yours already explained this all to you?"

"No, she hasn't," said Will, almost irritated.

"Well then, it's not my place to tell you. Sorry."

Bailey gave the queen a red-hot stare. "Tell us. We've waited too long for nothing." But then, she quickly backed down. "I mean, please, if you would."

"You dare raise your voice to me! Have we not given you water to quench your thirst or a bed to lay your ungrateful head in? Our land has been around for many a year. Our arrows fly a distance farther than your unprepared mind can perceive. Don't start an argument you know you cannot win. Treachery against the Ará will not go unnoticed."

Enraged, Bailey clutched her necklace and ripped it off. She slowly transformed into her bear form. The queen stared at her.

It was like a moment of thought that you would think was trapped in ice. It was like when something is in your blind spot that you can almost see but not quite or when there was something you wanted to see, if it was interesting or not, but you were too scared to look.

"You didn't tell me you were one of us." The queen eyed the girl.

Bailey and Will wondered whether her glance was one of shock or defiance—or both.

"What did you say your last name was, dear?" The queen's smile shifted in and out repetitively.

"Wright."

All colour drained from the queen's face. She smiled strangely at Bailey but apparently still able to compose herself. She seemed to take a minute to look at Bailey, who wondered why the queen had a look of pity across her face.

"My lady?" Bailey asked out of respect.

But the queen suddenly closed her eyes, taking a deep quivering breath. It took a few seconds. Will and Bailey were afraid that they broke her and shared a look of worry.

"Sorry. I'm so sorry," said the queen, looking down while straightening her dress. "Just old age, I suppose."

Then Lady Ava walked away, and the somber feeling in the air was almost suffocating.

Chapter

Thirteen

With every step Red took, she cringed. The loud crunch of the forest floor beneath her feet echoed and bounced among the trees surrounding her. She held her bow against her shoulder, and her knuckles turned white with tension with every step she took. Her quiver hit her back as she walked, which caused her to turn quickly around, as if something or someone was behind her.

And then it came again—that sort of cry.

Red started to run toward it. As she ran, she imagined a hurt horse or bear lying across the leaves and dirt. Then she stopped, breathing loudly, her hand against her chest. She tripped over a rock and had to catch herself by leaning on a tree. The force of her fall ripped her cardigan. She knew she would have a nasty scratch, but adrenaline was enough to help her not feel anything for the moment.

Eleanor had taught Red a method to keep her from unwillingly using her gift; in this case, the weather was a vital factor. She closed her eyes and imagined a tree—not an ordinary everyday tree. No, this was different. It was a tree grown by the water of tears—not exactly sad tears, but tears of laughter and joy. The Watson children would play under a tree they grew up with. And wonderful games they would play, which almost always ended up with Will getting hit on the head by a branch or falling and breaking something.

Red laughed to herself. She opened her eyes and looked around. The crying stopped. She nervously peered over the large tree branches and carefully climbed over trees that had been split in half, lying horizontally on the ground. Red was afraid of what she would see, especially since she might not be able to help.

She didn't see anything but decided to check anyway.

There it was.

She stood there, shaking a bit. A chestnut brown horse with a wounded leg eyed her from the ground; his eyes were watery. Red ran over. She kneeled on the ground and started to pet the horse.

"I'm sorry, buddy," she said quietly. She took a piece of cloth from her torn cardigan and tied it gently on the horse's leg. "I brought this from home just in case."

The horse turned his head at Red, who smiled at him softly. His eyes were large, Red noticed, but they looked frightened and full of knowing. Red's smile slowly vanished.

"What's wrong?"

The horse neighed as quietly as he could. Red petted his mane. For some reason, she felt chills run down her back, and an eerie feeling washed over her like stolen wind. She stood up and took a few steps away from the horse. Then she stopped and reminded herself that she needed to stay with him.

"Incredible," said a voice behind her.

Red quickly, though gracefully, grabbed an arrow from her quiver and pointed it directly at the head of the creature that had suddenly appeared, causing the latter to not move a muscle.

A female night corpse stared down at Red, who showed no fear of Red's bow. Just as Red was about to run away, the monster grabbed her arm.

"No use running, dear," she said in a slithery voice. "The forest has eyes."

Red looked around, and her breath caught in her throat. She noticed movement surrounding the forest around them, as well as small glowing red lights.

Eyes.

Red twisted her arm nimbly. She kicked the monster and stumbled away, grabbing an arrow from her quiver as she did so. She pulled the bowstring as far as she could and aimed it at the monster's head, but for some reason, she couldn't shoot.

The night corpse only laughed, a snarled wrinkly laugh, and turned to face the hurt horse with his watery eyes. "That's your weakness. You care too much."

Red pulled the bowstring tighter. "Empathy isn't weakness just as ineligible power isn't strength."

"Don't patronize me, Watson. Just because you can use a bow your aunt gave you doesn't give you the higher ground. Don't forget you're not the only gifted here."

They moved around each other, but there weren't any unexpected movements. Red's arm burned, but still, something kept her from firing.

"I'm the only gifted here without a poisoned mind, and believe me, that's a strength you cannot win against, no matter how hard you and your foul breath try."

"You think you have everything locked in, that you understand everything about the world? I don't know what world you and your friends grew up in, but the Gifted Lands don't believe in mercy."

As Red backed away, she ended up tripping on a root sticking out of the ground. She looked up, and her fists jammed into the dirt. She couldn't feel the pinch of the small pieces of rocks and rough leaves. She stood up and slowly walked toward the night corpse, and as she did, the heavy boulders around her gradually crumbled into dust.

"That is *not* true," she said and was surprised to hear how icy her voice sounded. "The Gifted Lands are only like this because of Callum and monsters like you. You communicate by speaking some words of wisdom to shield your dark mind from the surface of what you believe is the truth. That current is bound to go somewhere, and if you choose the side of destruction, then it is sure to take you far off stream."

"Who's to say you're not doing the same?"

Red knew her own words were right, but night corpses had a way of sneaking into your mind like poison. It was foul and had no beauty—that evil that had no meaning in life. Then why were so many people tempted and lured by it? Was it all because of power?

Red sighed and picked up her bow and quiver, which had left her hands when she fell.

"I don't fear Callum. I don't fear you," Red said calmly. "You have no power against my mind, and I suggest you leave and take your blind words with you."

"You're a strong child, but strength will only get you so far." The night corpse smiled.

Red suddenly remembered the hurt horse. "You wicked creature! How could you do such a thing? For power? Is that your motivation? Is that what turned you into this?"

The night corpse ignored Red's questions and eyed the horse with no sympathy in her eyes. "Actually, this was all your fault."

It was Red's turn to laugh.

"So this is Elivar. I'm sure Lady Ava will be thrilled to see us again. Thanks to you and your *empathy*." The night corpse then disappeared into the shadows of the forest.

Red placed her hands over her mouth; she could taste blood and bits of bark and leaf. Tears sprang from her eyes and fell onto her cardigan. She shakily walked toward the horse.

"I promise I'll come back for you," she said, her voice quivering.

The horse shook his head and neighed. Red understood though tears formed in her eyes.

Then she ran as fast as she could out of the forest and into the busy village. She had to dodge some villagers and children playing and eventually made it to the castle. She barged in, but nobody was there. She ran to the north wing of the castle and into Eleanor's room. Eleanor was sitting in a chair by the fireplace, reading a book.

"My goodness, dear, what happened?" she said, standing up. She eyed Red with a shocked expression.

The girl had tracked mud in and had it all over her trousers. Plus, she had red eyes, was sweaty, and had tears on her cheeks.

"Come here, dear. Tell me what's wrong," said Eleanor in a soothing voice

Red swallowed hard, though she wasn't able to speak for a minute. She tried to talk and was eventually able to compose herself. She looked up into Eleanor's eyes, waiting for that look of disappointment she had always dreaded. But there was only a look of motherly worry.

"It's all my fault," said Red quietly.

"Well, I'm sure that, whatever it is, is not your fault," said Eleanor, laughing a little.

"I went to help an injured horse, and a night corpse was there, along with a whole mess of them in the shadows of the forest. I argued with her for a while. And then she told me they were going to destroy Elivar, and that it was all my fault." Red cried into her aunt's shoulder. A lump was growing in her throat.

"Red, look at me in my eyes," said Eleanor, grabbing her niece's hands. "Breathe. And listen to rationality."

Red took a minute to breathe. She instantly felt better. Her eyes dried up, but her hands were still sweaty. She sighed and looked up to see not a disappointed look but a smile.

"It's not your fault. Night corpses have a way of making you think everything is your doing. That's why they are so dangerous," Eleanor said. Then she turned her head anxiously. "I have to alert Lady Ava. Red, get your siblings and Bailey, lock this door, and then use anything to barricade it. Am I clear?"

Red nodded furiously and ran out the door without hesitation. Eleanor did the same.

—⟋⟍—

Lady Ava was in the village's garden. She sat on a stone bench and looked as if she were asleep. Eleanor ran toward her, which startled the queen.

"What is it, Watson?" Lady Ava said, glaring at Eleanor.

"You must prepare for an invasion, my lady. Night corpses—and possibly Callum—are on their way here. They are many." Eleanor was out of breath.

Lady Ava stared at Eleanor. Then she stood up and grabbed Eleanor's shoulder.

"Is what you say true, Watson?" Her icy eyes were replaced with steaming eyes of fury. "Shall we prepare for war?"

"Not war. There will be no need for it if Elivar is as well minded as they say they are," said Eleanor shortly.

"Very well. Please lead the townsfolk and yourself into the cellar below the castle," said the queen.

But when Eleanor nodded and started to run, Lady Ava grabbed her shoulder again and said in a low voice, "Prepare your mind."

Then the queen slowly turned into a snowy owl and flew toward the castle. Eleanor's shoulder started throbbing. She looked toward the distant sky and then ran toward the village.

It was not silent. Though orders of silence were called for, nobody listened. Eleanor watched as Arás shape-shifted, trying to escape. But they eventually didn't leave because they didn't want to abandon their families or their country.

"Everyone, follow me!" Eleanor yelled as loudly as she possibly could. "By order of the queen, you are to follow my directions!"

The villagers followed Eleanor in a somewhat neat line. They reached the castle, and there was a stampede of worried eyes and terrified cries of both children and adults who ran past the castle doors. Eleanor could only watch as the younger children held on to their mother's arms in blunt ignorance.

Once everyone was in the castle's cellar, soldiers aged fifteen and up grabbed a sword or a bow and proceeded beyond the country's gate. Eleanor followed the line and grabbed a beautifully crafted sword, but she was stopped by a hand.

"I am sorry, but you know you are too old for battle. Think about your nieces and nephew. Red needs you. She is *very* powerful, Eleanor," said Lady Ava, a look of pity in her eyes.

Eleanor pulled her arm away. "I am perfectly capable of handling myself, my lady."

"Don't just think about yourself. I also need you to stay with the townsfolk and keep them calm and protected."

Eleanor turned away but agreed. Lady Ava cleared her throat. "The Wright family's daughter is with you. I didn't recognize her. She's growing suspicious. Have you told her anything?"

Eleanor shook her head. "She shouldn't know anything. I don't think she's ready. But with my nieces and nephew here, especially Red, I suspect it will be much easier for her to find out."

Lady Ava sighed. "Stay safe, Eleanor."

Eleanor nodded. "You as well."

—◊◊—

Red ran down a stone path toward the stables but ran into someone, which caused her to fall onto her back. A familiar face helped her up, and her name was called repeatedly.

"Red! Red! Are you okay?" asked a worried Will. "I am so sorry. I didn't see you."

Red smiled through the pain and hugged her brother. "I am so happy to see you after the day I just had."

Will smiled. "I don't know what that means, but alright."

Suddenly remembering her task, Red looked at her brother with sudden seriousness.

"I need you to help me find Claire and Bailey. We need to get to Aunt Eleanor's room quickly. I'll explain on the way."

Fourteen

A strong wind came that evening. Red, Claire, Will, and Bailey were locked away in their room. The silence was hard to listen to, but no one wanted to make any noise even if it couldn't be heard. Red was tired and felt as if she were half asleep.

"We'll be alright," she said with a splash of optimism. "This is Elivar, the strongest country when it comes to battle strategy. And I trust Aunt Eleanor."

That just made the others more worried.

Claire looked up at Red, her eyes conveying her worry. "I really hope Aunt Eleanor's alright and that they don't make her fight."

A wave of worry crashed over Red's mind. She sighed deeply and watched as her siblings and friend sat there in silence and worry. There was nothing she could do to comfort them.

Then she stood up from her bed and walked over to them, who were sitting in a half circle. She took a seat in between Claire and Will and put an arm on each of their shoulders while giving a warm and comforting but a bit worrisome smile to Bailey. They all appreciated it more than Red might have thought.

Sometimes there's just nothing we can say to make people feel better, Red thought, *but a little hope sure does help.*

—⟋∭⟍—

It was freezing, and a supply of blankets were passed around in case of emergencies. There were no soldiers to calm the terrified townsfolk, only an older woman with a warm and charming smile. Eleanor knew she had to try, though she was afraid herself, very much so.

"This is all because of you and your family," said a voice a little farther into the cellar.

Eleanor peered over to see a woman carrying a baby, sitting next to her husband and a young boy.

The woman continued, "Those monsters are only coming here because of your arrival. And that Watson girl—gifted folk are always so unpredictable. You can never trust them, especially nowadays."

Eleanor tried to ignore the hurt and anger bubbling in her stomach. "I assure you we don't mean you or anyone any harm. We had nowhere to go, and 'that Watson girl' is actually the one destined to save us all from Callum's reign."

"Really?" said another voice, but it wasn't said in a curious cheerful voice, quite the opposite actually. It came from a young man around nineteen who sat next to a young girl whom Eleanor guessed was his sister.

"Why must we trust a few extremely powerful gifted? The Ará has done perfectly fine without the need of excessive power," the young man asked.

Eleanor bit her lip. The taste of blood wasn't nearly as salty as the words of the townsfolk—and didn't hurt quite as much.

Silence.

Some children started getting restless, while others started getting more scared by the minute. Eleanor watched as they sniffled; the smaller ones clung to stuffed animals and their parents' hands. She did the only thing she could. She started singing a beautiful song in Gaelic. The words weren't ripe but were perfectly poised and balanced like a timed dance of swans along a nimble river.

Nuair a laigh grian an fheasgair taobh thall na beinne. Nochdaidh Uisge domhainn. Lorgaidh solas na h-uinneigh agus aoibhneas an fheòir a shlighe fo shnaigheadh craobh daraich. Ma stadas an t-eagal seasamh nas fhaide ann am mionaid.

Nì mi gàirdeachas. O, seallaidh cridhe nas fhaide na glainne, a 'mhadainn bhuidhe bhuidhe. Nuair a laigh grian an fheasgair taobh thall na beinne. Seinnidh mi mo dhàn dhut, a ghràidh. Dìreach feitheamh ris an mac-talla

a shlighe a lorg dhut agus seinnidh e fad na sìorraidheachd.

People stared, while some whispered. The children eyed her with curiosity. Some even walked up to where she was sitting and plopped themselves onto the floor next to her.

Eleanor sang with more joy. Maybe it was the faces of young hearts surrounding her that caused her to forget any trouble she had ever known. And it was this moment that made her believe that good would always be holding on.

The Ará still eyed her like she was going to get them killed, even if the cellar *was* soundproof. Some decided to sit alongside the children and, to Eleanor's surprise, even knew some of the words.

When Eleanor finished, people clapped as quietly as they could, and the children pleaded for more. Eleanor smiled down at the wonderful faces and sang a special song in Elivar's own tongue, Elivarian. Even more joined in, and everyone knew the words this time.

Pretty soon, nobody seemed to remember where they were.

—◆—

The rain was quiet yet deafening.

Lady Ava stood in waiting at the front of the gate in Elivar. She looked back toward the village about a quarter of a mile behind her, searching for tiny lights from torches that would indicate their position.

All the Ará that could shape-shift into dangerous animals were kept in the shadows near the gate.

The queen turned to face the gate, and she gasped quietly as a tall man came forward and stood before her.

Callum looked terrible. He had regained his power, but he also regained his night corpse appearance. And he looked much worse than he did before his powers had been sealed.

Lady Ava glared at him. "If it isn't Callum, the treacherous prince. And without an army, I see," she said coldly. "This is a surprise."

"I don't need an army," said Callum. "I wonder, my lady, why are you standing out here in the rain, waiting?"

Lady Ava said nothing for a few seconds. She only glared at his horrid eyes. "And why, I must ask, are *you* here?"

Callum's smile was twisted, and his crooked teeth peeked from his open mouth. "I must say, my lady, your people are very skilled at hiding. For many years, we have hunted the Ará, and now because of Red Watson, we have finally found you."

Lady Ava tightened her grip on her sword. "Don't blame the child. Night corpses are very good at trickery, and I don't suppose you use that to your advantage."

"We're not here to fight, Ava. We just want your country, and we'll be right out. So here are the options." He held up two fingers, indicating two choices. "You risk your country for nothing, or you save your country by handing it over. As a wise queen, I am sure you'll make the right decision for your people."

Lady Ava closed her eyes. "Very well," she said, "follow me."

Callum laughed. "And when I follow you, guards will start attacking us? No, I am good. Thank you."

"Alright then," the queen said, not a trace of impatience in her voice. "Here are *your* options." She, too, held up two fingers. "You stay here, call battle on us, and lose your whole army. Or you come with me to get our divine flower, and nobody gets hurt."

Callum smiled at the words *divine flower.* "The flower of your country will seal the deal. But listen here, Ava. If anything happens, I'm not afraid to announce war. I'd like to see what a country of ducks and rabbits will do against my army of monsters."

"Come," Lady Ava said and started walking toward the village. Her mind ached slightly, like she was missing something. She spotted a few torches and searched her mind for any ideas. "We need light. I shall make us a torch."

She grabbed a piece of wood from the ground and lit the top of it with two other pieces. Callum ignored her unethical method. Lady Ava lifted her torch and swayed it ever so slightly, which then received an answer of lights before her. She only did so when Callum looked away for just a moment. Lady Ava watched as he stepped on every flower without looking down at his feet.

"Just over here," she said, walking to the rear of the castle, where the previous torches had signaled to her.

Callum placed a hand on her shoulder. "Are you sure?"

Lady Ava stopped. She could feel her heart almost screaming to get away. She could feel it talking, murmuring, and frantically attempting just some kind of communication. But the queen just stared down at the grass.

"Right," she said, smoothing her dress. "This way."

They entered the castle.

Lady Ava opened a door with several locks that opened to a staircase. She knew how much Callum needed that flower, so she wasn't worried about his conviction. Though her heart seemed to be beating louder as if it was trying to wake up her mind, she ignored it.

They reached a door.

"If you think I will announce Arthur's request, then you really are a fool," said Callum, glaring at Lady Ava. "You better be true to your word. I am not someone to make a bargain with lightly."

"If you really think I'd use something so futile, then you're the fool," she countered.

Lady Ava opened the lock with a silver key. Then she gestured for them to enter the room. Callum hesitated but still eventually entered. Inside was a beautiful flower sitting upright in a glass container.

Callum eyed it intensely. "All these years, and here it is right in front of my eyes—one of the keys to finish it all."

Lady Ava listened, but she wasn't sure if Callum knew that she was. She pulled a hidden lever on the side of the wall; it was in a shadowy part not visible to the human eye, unless you were looking for it. Steel bars fell fast below their cage, trapping Callum. But he didn't notice this until a few seconds after.

Lady Ava sighed. "I honestly thought you had become wiser. You were always so naïve, even as an adult. You have disappointed me in so many ways, and I'm sure your family wasn't thrilled either."

"You are the naïve one," said Callum, his voice sounding slightly more high-pitched.

"What are you talking about, you monster?" Lady Ava said, reaching for her sword.

Callum slowly turned into a less-nasty-looking but still disgusting creature—a night corpse.

Lady Ava stared at him in surprise, anger, and disgust. Her ice-cold eyes glared at him as she screamed, "That wicked charlatan!" She threw her sword onto the wall, and it stuck deep in it. Then she strode toward the night corpse and demanded, "Listen to me, creature. What is your leader planning?"

"And why would I tell you?" He laughed at her mockingly. "Why would I risk a painful death from our master?"

"Trust me. That will happen anyway. But speak, and you might be of use for a while." Lady Ava spoke in a tone with obvious abhorrence and proceeded to pick up her sword.

The night corpse looked down. "Useful? How?"

Lady Ava didn't answer. She took her sword and left the room, hatred bubbling in her heart.

—‍⟪‍—

"I should have known. The monster made me believe that my foolish plan of luring him in by myself would work. Now I lower my head in shame. It is my fault." Lady Ava watched the village from the window of Eleanor's room. "I promised myself I wouldn't make the same mistake."

"Don't blame yourself," said Eleanor. "If they want to, night corpses can make someone believe a rock is brilliant."

Red stood near her aunt, who had asked her to stay with her. "So it wasn't Callum, just a night corpse?"

"*Just* a night corpse?" the queen repeated, a hint of sarcasm upon her lips. "Do not underestimate a night corpse. You need to have an extremely powerful heart and an especially steady mind to survive a confrontation with one without being tricked or feeling terrible afterward. It takes many decades of practice to build up strength to counter them."

Red looked down, embarrassed.

Eleanor noticed this, and she placed a hand on her niece's shoulder. "You did much better than me when I first encountered one." She winked at her.

Red looked up at her. "But wasn't my first time at the inn?"

"That's different, dear. You were with Mr. Stone," said Eleanor bluntly.

"I fear Callum is planning something big," said Lady Ava. She kept her gaze out the window. "I don't know if Elivar is ready, but we'll prepare for battle."

Red looked up at the queen. "But Elivar has been around for centuries of blue moons. Surely you're ready."

Lady Ava closed her eyes. "Get some rest. You all leave at first light. It's too much of a risk to keep you here." She turned toward Red and placed a firm hand on her shoulder. "I have faith in you, young gifted. And remember to use your power wisely. Controlling the weather is one of the smallest abilities you have. You'll discover more as you go— hopefully, not the hard way."

Red nodded, though she only understood half of what the queen told her. She fell asleep instantly, right when her head hit her pillow.

—⁂—

Everything was pitch-black. Something smelled of dead fish and seaweed. And it was wet.

Odd.

Red could also taste something. It was salty and bitter. She tried moving, yet it felt almost restricting. She looked down. She was completely submerged, from her shoulders down, in water. She tried treading it, but her arms ached after a few minutes. She gasped for air, but her lungs felt weak.

Not once did she wonder why she was in an ocean.

It felt like hours of constant worry and more treading water. She was tired, and her body screamed for her to rest. But as she did, she became submerged in water from her chin down. For some reason, the water was becoming saltier by the minute. As she glanced at her last view of sky, she saw light reflecting off the water.

"Give me your hand," said a voice from above the water.

Though Red wondered why she could hear it so clearly since her ears were underwater, she still reached out with all her strength and grabbed the hand. She was pulled onto land, which miraculously appeared out of thin air. She lay on her back, which ached along with her entire body. Her eyes burning from the salty water, so she couldn't open them fully.

"Sit down here with me, Red. Let's have some tea," said the voice in a jolly manner. "Don't be afraid, dear."

Red stood up to see Mr. Stone sitting in an armchair from his inn. There was an identical one, which was empty, next to him. Red gasped, though not for air this time.

"Mr. Stone!" She smiled. "How are you here? How am *I* here?"

Mr. Stone just laughed. He poured Red some water and handed the cup to her. She eyed it like it was the last thing she wanted to deal with at that moment. Still, she took it and stared at it, not knowing what to say.

"Don't worry. It's salt-free," he said. Then he handed her tea. He looked up at the many stars above them. "Have you ever taken a minute to appreciate the beauty of nature?"

Red thought about it and nodded. "I've always loved trees," she said, which got a cheerful smile of agreement from Mr. Stone. Red looked down at the water around her and sighed.

"What's wrong, my child?"

"I'm scared." Red was afraid to talk. "I've always admired being courageous, and I show it sometimes. But lately I've had a hard time feeling it. Everything just feels like it's happening too soon and that I've done something wrong. I just hope I can make Aunt Eleanor, my family, and you proud. I'm just afraid this power is too much for me to handle."

"Don't feel like all this is your doing." Mr. Stone drank some of his tea. "Being human means being weak, but it also means having the choice of being courageous in order to be better. Don't underestimate yourself, especially since I don't. Remember what I said at my inn? I see a courageous young woman who will restore the Gifted Lands. My dear, I will not lie to you. This path will only get harder, but it will be worth it. Plus, you have your family to guide you, which will make things a lot easier to handle."

Red smiled. She felt a wonderful feeling down in her bones, which she felt was simply unexplainable. She gave Mr. Stone a hug.

"Thank you," she said.

Mr. Stone looked Red in the eye, and she noticed that his eyes sparkled and had a warm bright feeling to them.

He said, "Always remember to stay safe. You will be alright. But when all else fails, turn to the sun in its blinding glory, for it will guide you."

—⁂—

Red opened her eyes to see Eleanor staring down at her.

Eleanor said, "Come on, dear. We have to get going. Lady Ava said we could borrow two horses and a brougham. We'll cover distance twice as fast."

Red placed a hand on her head. "I had the strangest dream—but strange in the best way possible. Mr. Stone was there, and he helped me feel better about everything. It didn't even feel like a dream."

Eleanor smiled. "That's interesting, dear."

Red expected her aunt to ask her many follow-up questions, but all Eleanor did was fold clothes and put them in a small luggage.

"I feel bad about leaving right when they're getting ready for battle." Red still felt like it was her fault, yet she kept that to herself.

Eleanor took a seat on the bed next to Red. "Remember, this is Elivar. They have survived many a war with their smarts. We can't let Callum find us, mo ghràdh, especially you. This is better for everyone."

By the time they reached the gate of Elivar, Lady Ava looked over at them with that signature Elivarian half-smile on her lips. This time, it felt more genuine.

Red watched the horse-drawn carriage as she also discovered her newfound courage.

Chapter

Fifteen

The road the group took was bumpy and dull. It had been many hours, and sunlight was nearing its end. Eleanor constantly looked toward the side of the brougham. An Ará was at the driver's seat. He was an older man with a top hat and a monotone expression plastered across his tired face.

"*Maitheas*, goodness," mumbled Eleanor, "*chan eil earbsa agam anns a' choille seo.*"

Red listened to her aunt, wishing she understood.

"I don't trust the forest either," the Ará said with a faint accent.

Eleanor looked surprised. "I've never met an Ará who can speak Gaelic so well." She smiled, though there was still a hint of worry in her voice.

The Ará smiled—or half-smiled. "I grew up in Glasgow. My father was an Ará, so we moved to Elivar when I was eleven." He kept his gaze on the road, apparently sharing the same suspicion as Eleanor. "I fear what that corrupted prince is capable of. Being locked up all these years, he must be angry."

Bailey looked away quickly.

"Lady Ava said something about that too," Will said. "Why does everyone keep calling Callum a prince?"

Eleanor pursed her lips. "Well," she said, holding her hands together, "Callum *was* a prince. When Arthur, Callum, and I were young, he was prince of the Gifted Land Country, and his father was the king."

"Not the rightful king, I'll say," said the Ará, "but a good ruler. I'll give him that."

"What does he mean?" asked Red.

"A long while ago, the line of heirs was cut off after the old king died with no descendants or distant relatives, but it didn't matter. There may have been kings and queens, but none were the real heirs. The true king left many, many centuries before, and he left his throne for a peasant to take over. Nobody knew why he did such a thing. When Callum found out, it enraged him, and when he tried to prove his worth to the world, he became . . . well, he became how he is now. It just took a while for me to see the difference since we were very close friends."

Eleanor turned her head. "Never mind that. We mustn't linger on this topic for long. Would it be alright if we went quicker?" she asked the Ará, who lifted his hat in agreement.

"Where are we going, anyway?" asked Will. He shuffled his knees and feet as he spoke. "It's not that much longer, is it?"

"Calm down, William. Patience. Our goal is to get to Wildur for information on Callum. Then we'll plan from there. You will get to sleep in a tree."

"Really?" Red shouted without realizing it. "That's wonderful!"

"It would be if you were a bird." Claire smiled at her sister. "I don't think I'd fancy staying in a tree."

"Not all houses in Wildur are like that, dear." Eleanor laughed. "Wildur folks are quite the opposite of Elivar. While the Ará are quite a conservative race, Wildur folks are very hospitable. But they are easily afraid, hence the trees. And I just might make us stay in one to help you with that fear."

Claire slumped down in her seat and then proceeded to look out the window. Red noticed small groups of dust scattered across the frame of the window, but the view was beautiful. It was a maze of gilded flowers, roses, and sunflowers, and it was green as far as the eye could see. The trees had limbs that seemed to stretch toward the sun, accompanied by leaves of all colours, for it was the middle of autumn.

By night, it became very cold. Eleanor said it felt like the cellar or maybe even colder. Suddenly, the horses neighed and stomped their hooves, abruptly stopping the carriage, which caused everyone to bump into each other.

"What happened?" asked Eleanor.

She tapped the Ará on the shoulder but got no reply. He just pointed a shaky finger.

In front of them were three wolves with bloodred eyes and sharp claws. They looked beat up and had many deep scars and missing fur.

Looking at them, Red almost felt like throwing up. She looked around for anything useful.

"Aunt Eleanor," she whispered, "use the lanterns. Throw them at them."

Eleanor shook her head—well, as much as she could at the moment. Her neck hurt from constantly turning to check behind the carriage. "We need it for something else." She carefully tried reaching for the lantern, with no help from the Ará.

"Almost there," she said, and everyone held their breath as they watched her.

Eleanor successfully retrieved one of the lanterns and tried reaching for the second, but one of the wolves crept closer. Red noticed it was missing an eye.

"Go away! What do you want? I've only got four pence in my pocket!" Will tried shooing it away. "Why aren't they responding? I thought animals could talk here or something."

Eleanor tried her best not to scold her nephew but still ended up berating him. "Sit down, William! I better not hear another peep out of you."

Will nodded frantically as Eleanor whispered instructions to the Ará, who might or might not have been listening. Will looked to Bailey with a look of either worry or anger, Red couldn't decide.

"Hey! Why don't you turn into a bear?" said Will, having forgotten Eleanor's command almost instantly.

Eleanor glared at her nephew, and he retreated back and stared awkwardly out the window.

Bailey opened her hands, which had been cupped tightly for the whole trip. A ripped necklace was lying in her quivering fingers. She threw it on the floor but eventually picked it up again and held it against her heart.

"If I wasn't so careless, if I just had any thought in my head at all, this wouldn't have happened," Bailey said quietly, almost to herself.

Eleanor gave her a look of pity, though she couldn't look away from the wolves. "We'll talk later, dear," she said. Then she tried tapping the Ará on the shoulder again, to no avail. She huffed and then opened the side door carefully.

"Stop!" said Claire. But then she saw the look of determination on Eleanor's face. "Just be careful, please," she said apprehensively.

Eleanor walked out slowly. She made no sound and kept within the shadows. She held one lantern close to her face; the other stayed inside the carriage.

The wolves howled and stomped and circled the brougham. Eleanor closed her eyes as she kept her distance from them. She finally made her way behind the wolves, gently lowered the lantern down, and placed her hands on the soil. Suddenly, roots grew fast from the ground and silently wrapped themselves around the wolves. As they closed around the wolves tightly, the howls were muffled.

The company cheered, Will stuck his head out of the brougham, lantern in hand. He tossed it toward the branches, which was followed by a cry of anger from the group.

"You fool!" Red said, grabbing Will's sleeve and pulling him back into the brougham. "Do you realize what you have done?"

Eleanor retreated quickly back into the carriage, her face filled with horror. She shook the Ará as gently as she could, and he awoke from shock with a gasp. He grabbed the reins and led the horses speeding around the bundle of burning roots and at twice the speed. They looked back and saw a large fire and smoke surrounding it.

Will turned back to his family, who all gave him the death stare.

"I'm sorry. I didn't realize—" he started.

"No, you didn't, William," said Eleanor, no trace of sympathy in her voice. "You have attracted the enemy with a fire like that, and I'm sure many night corpses and other wolves and monsters will be one our path any time soon."

Will simply stared at his feet, but the intense feeling of guilt was searing in his chest. It burned almost as much as the fire nearby, which the group could feel hot on their necks. The blinding wave of smoke became more distant as they rode farther away.

"Will the branches hold them?" asked Red, looking back at the trapped wolves.

"I'm not at all saying that the fire was a good idea, but it will certainly kill off all the wolves. I suppose we got a couple of hours before any enemies find it, but we'll be far from here by that time," said Eleanor.

Red looked up at her aunt. Suddenly, she remembered something. "Aunt Eleanor, what about that meeting we were supposed to have when we first left your mansion?"

Eleanor sighed lightly. "To be most frank, there was no meeting. I just didn't want to give you all a fright. Those two people you overheard me talking to are part of a kind of council. They had informed me of danger, so I figured it was time for us to start this journey. That letter I sent at the inn was just to fill them in on our situation."

Red couldn't be angry with her aunt. "I understand," she said. She felt a pang of hurt deep inside, but she hid it well.

Not long later, she spotted a dove sitting by a lantern. He had soft eyes that felt calm and serene. She shifted her body in her seat but still felt the gaze of the bird on her.

Where do I know you from? Red thought as she kept her gaze on the dove.

Eleanor's anger at Will was still fresh in her heart, but she noticed Red's behavior. She placed a hand on Red's knee, which was her way of telling her niece to relax.

"I don't plan on staying for too long. We'll have to stay a night, but we will only visit the Wildur Library. I trust you all will stay safe and sensible," said Eleanor.

Both Red and Will suspected it was directed toward them.

"Yes, Aunt Eleanor," they said simultaneously.

The dove turned his head and flew toward the window near Red. She had to admit he was a very majestic animal. Something about his eyes was familiar in an odd way. If only she could remember . . . It was in her "blind spot," far from reach.

"There's a dove," said Red, not exactly knowing how to explain, "and I feel like it's trying to tell me something."

Claire peered over to see the dove plainly staring at Red. "Odd. Doves rarely fancy people, let alone be around them. I wonder if it's an Ará."

Red suddenly felt a slight chill slide down her spine. She looked over at the window, but the dove had already left. She held her cardigan sleeves tightly with the palms of her hands, which were a tad sweaty, and tried to fall asleep. It was uncomfortable and strange; the best word she could use was *odd*.

— ∞ —

"Over here!" said a night corpse. "This is where we saw the fire."

A group of night corpses emerged from the shadows of the night. They had spotted the large fire and quickly made their way on foot toward it. It smelled very foul.

One of them started sniffing the area, while the others felt the fire. Night corpses couldn't feel the burn of fire, so it had no effect on them.

"Where did they go?" another roared.

"We must search everywhere! He told us not to fail this time, and you all know what happens when he gets angry."

The monsters did search everywhere—under rocks, behind trees. Then one smaller night corpse jumped with joy as he picked up a shattered lantern.

"Hey! Hey! I found something!" he yelled.

"Look at those markings," said a larger night corpse, who quickly snatched it. "This is from Elivar. You don't suppose the Watson girl left Elivar in a rush and happened to . . ." He searched the dirt below him and eventually found scattered tree branches and deep claw marks. "Wolves."

"What shall we do?" asked the small night corpse.

Before the large night Corpse could answer, a dove fluttered down from a branch above. The night corpses eyed it with confusion and hints of amusement.

"Hullo, little birdy!" said one. "Come down, and I'll turn you into dove soup!"

The dove descended to the ground, and as he did, he turned into a man with calm, unwavering eyes. He was holding a sword against his chest.

"By the power of the sun, you shall return to your torture of solitude in the darkness. You are not worthy of breathing our fresh air. Leave, foul beasts!"

The night corpses walked toward the man. As they pulled out their swords, their eyes became a deep red.

The man fought them gracefully. His feet seemed to dance as he swung his weapon left and right. The night corpses would shriek and cry as they felt the grueling pain of the sword. Though night corpses were great fighters, this man made them look like children playing with form swords.

Eventually, there were no more night corpses left, except for one. The small night corpse had his back against a large rock, and he was breathing heavily.

"Please," said the night corpse quietly.

The man looked down at his eyes. They were not as red as the others. The night corpse quivered in fear.

The man reached a hand down at him. "Cease your weeping. Take my hand if you wish, but remember, you will no longer be as you were before."

The night corpse looked up at the man, and tears welled up in his eyes. He grabbed the offered hand, and the man pulled him up. The night corpse was heavy, as they all were, for the weight of guilt, hurt, and betrayal was a very heavy burden. But as the man pulled him up, the night corpse changed into a human. He was not gifted anymore, but he was free.

"Thank you," he said. "Thank you."

The man nodded, his warm smile accompanied by cheerful eyes. He walked away, and as he did, the marks of the wolves slowly disappeared and were replaced by a single white flower.

—m—

If words are just a distraction from the truth, then everything must be overused and busy. These were the thoughts Red would get occasionally, a trait she inherited from Eleanor. One of Red's favourites was "What the heart seeks can either be blurred or blunt but nothing in between," which was something Eleanor would tell her.

Red smiled to herself. She could hear Eleanor's voice inside her head, which gradually turned into her singing. It was so loud and clear that Red turned her head a couple of times to see if her aunt really was singing.

The notes were perfectly balanced, straight on point, like they were flowing down a waterfall and into the clear river. It was calling her to sing along. Red could hear her name, though she didn't bother opening her eyes to check. She just listened and nodded along to the melody.

"Red!" said Will, shaking his sister until she stared up at him, confused. "We've been calling your name for five minutes! We're here."

Red looked outside her window. There were so many joyful villagers, and it was quite the opposite of Elivar. For Wildur folk seemed genuinely excited despite not having as much as Elivar. The town buildings were something one could see in a book of medieval architecture, like mostly everything in the Gifted Lands. Red was completely starstruck and had to be dragged out of the brougham by Claire.

"Welcome to Wildur. I must meet with Peter Silver, the mayor, to discuss where he wants to put us. I have asked his children to give you all a short tour, and I expect everyone to come back safe," said Eleanor. She gave them all a quick hug and headed toward a busy part of the village.

Two villagers walked up to them, seemingly arguing with each other. They looked about the same age as Red and her siblings. One was a tall, skinny boy with wavy dark brown hair and blue eyes. The other was a girl who was a bit shorter and had wavy strawberry-blonde hair and brown eyes. Both wore amazingly detailed outfits Red felt she had seen in a medieval-themed book. She laughed slightly to herself, as she they reminded her of Hansel and Gretel.

Their faces lit up as soon as they saw the group.

"It's really you!" said the girl, whom Red noticed was looking straight at her. "You're Red Watson, are you not?"

Red nodded. She wasn't used to people recognizing her, especially people she hadn't met before. The girl turned toward her brother and grinned.

"Our names are Matilda and Benjamin—or Tilly and Ben—and we're very glad that you all are visiting Wildur," Tilly said.

The others wondered how she could speak without taking a breath every once in a while.

"My sister gets excited for everything, but we really are happy to see you all," said Ben. He lifted his hand for the others to shake, as did his sister. He continued, "We never get any outsiders to visit us."

Red couldn't imagine why. Wildur wasn't like Elivar, which was known for how conservative and locked up they were. She shook their hands, and so her companions. Bailey seemed a bit more untrusting as she quickly shook the siblings' hands.

"Follow us. We only have an hour to show you everything amazing about Wildur," said Tilly, seemingly stressed out by this fact.

They headed toward a small forest, which Red was a little nervous about. She hated that—the fact that she was nervous about a forest. But an encounter with a night corpse was hard to recover from, and Red tried her best to find courage.

—⚏—

Eleanor reached a wooden cottage. It looked very cozy, and she appreciated this more than the castle in Elivar. She knocked on the door and waited a couple of minutes for a reply. The door was opened by a tall man with dark brown hair and a sky-blue overcoat. He had friendly eyes and a kind smile.

"Why, good day there, miss. What can I help you with?" he asked.

Eleanor smiled on the outside, a little disappointed she wasn't recognized by him. "I am Eleanor Watson, a close friend of Arthur Wildur."

"Ah, I see," said the man. "What brings you to Wildur?"

Eleanor was bewildered. "Hasn't Lady Ava told you of our arrival, Mr. Silver?"

The man smiled. "Oh, you mean my brother, Peter. Yes, I will get him. Come on in, Ms. Watson. Have some tea."

Eleanor walked inside the cottage, which was a lot bigger on the inside. She was shocked and stood in her place for more than a few minutes. The man laughed proudly and poured her some tea.

"It really never gets old," he said. "My name is Oliver." He shook Eleanor's hand and then disappeared into a hallway.

Oliver came back moments later with a man who looked only a couple of years older than him. He was wearing the same style of overcoat as his brother's, yet his was a moss green.

Eleanor stood up to greet him with a smile. "Mr. Silver, it's a pleasure to meet you."

Peter had a warm smile on his face. "The pleasure is all mine, especially to a good friend of Arthur Wildur."

Eleanor beamed, exhaling with relief. She took a seat on a small couch, and the others did the same.

"Well, I was meaning to ask you, Mr. Silver, on where my group can stay for the night, but . . ." Eleanor looked down at her shoes, not able to make eye contact with Peter for some unknown reason. "If you don't mind, I want to ask if any of you may have any clue on the whereabouts of my dear friend." She prepared herself. She already knew their answer and didn't really want to feel the hurt of disappointment, but she couldn't really help asking.

"Well," started Peter, "we have one thing. It's not much, but maybe, since you knew him, you could figure it out." He stood up and walked toward a beautiful wooden bookshelf. From there, he took out a scroll and handed it to her.

Eleanor took it without hesitation. As she held it, she felt almost scared to see what was inside. She forced herself to open the scroll and then stared blankly at it for a few seconds. She read it out loud, and her heart drank each word.

> *I've closed my eyes about a million times now. I can feel it*
> *in the earth and in the water. The advice from the king is*
> *overwhelming but enough to sort me out. I fear leaving, but*
> *everything I see looks different now. If anyone has the need*
> *for my assistance, my request will live as it may, a memory*
> *of words that have left their mark upon the shadows of the*

sun's rays, a symbol of my gratitude opened upon the one. But I am not the one I have so wholeheartedly believed myself to be. It is another.

I have been told that, years from now, there will be someone courageous enough to overcome what we all fear most, and Callum is only a fraction of it. There will be that time of peace, but for now, I must rely on my mind, not my heart, which I wish should not be the way.

—AW

Eleanor held the scroll tightly in her quivering hands. She could hear her dear friend's voice as she read his words. She had to read the scroll again to retain anything because the first time she read it, the shock prevented her from seeing anything but words on a paper.

"Anything, Ms. Watson?" asked Oliver, his voice muffled under the rim of his teacup.

Eleanor read and reread the scroll, but she kept her eye on one line: "If anyone has the need for my assistance, my request will live as it may, a memory of words that have left their mark upon the shadows of the sun's rays, a symbol of my gratitude opened upon the one."

She looked up at the brothers, her eyes welling up with tears, and said solemnly, "I just may."

Chapter

Sixteen

Red couldn't deny that it was a stunning forest. There were small ponds and stones that caught the sun's rays perfectly. It felt great. Red placed a hand on her heart; she felt like everything was healing already.

They had a wonderful time in the forest. When they passed a river, Will fell in and gave everyone a good laugh. He wasn't too thrilled about it, which made it more amusing. They found many creatures, including animals that rose from the water—and in liquid shape.

"They are called river fauna. They originated from Tìr an Uisge and spread from there. Ours were a gift from Elivar—before everything happened," said Ben.

Red watched as water from a nearby river slowly morphed into the shape of a rabbit. It hopped toward her, and she attempted to pet it. The rabbit still felt like water but more firm. It then hopped back into the river and disappeared.

"Remarkable," said Claire, who was holding a sketchbook. "I've never seen anything even slightly like them."

"The Gifted Lands contain many remarkable creatures, which is why we do our very best to protect them. This forest is guarded every day, not just for the animals," said Tilly, her voice going down a few octaves as her eyes wandered off. Then she shook her head. "Never mind that."

Her perky spirit returned, and she led the group out of the forest, much to Red's disappointment.

There were bakers and plays and puppet shows. The flower shops had an array of beautiful flowers. To Red, never had the world been this beautiful. Maybe it was just that feeling in the pit of her stomach, or maybe it was the look on every villager's face? This joy was something Red saw occasionally in London, though not in this magnitude.

"Let's visit Mr. Ivansgrove. He's this town's bookshop owner and our godfather. He occasionally lends me books when he's in a good mood, which he always is," said Tilly.

She skipped ahead a few paces, leaving everyone else in a frenzy to catch up with her.

The way Claire felt as she walked into the bookshop was the same as what Red felt in the forest. It was miraculous how people could be the same but also entirely different, sometimes at the same time. Red looked around the bookshop. She felt that the warm feeling was very inviting.

As soon as one stepped inside, the first thing one would notice was the walls lined with books and shelves with rocks and figurines. There were also beautiful artwork and vases full of colourful flowers. The ceiling was so high one had to tilt one's head until it hurt just to see it—and even almost fall backward.

Red loved everything about Wildur.

"Why, if it isn't little Tilly and Ben!" said a voice from across the room, which echoed slightly.

A man walked into the room. He had a graying beard and a white cardigan, and he held a tower of books in his hands as he struggled to get them to a nearby table. Red helped him carry them. As soon as he saw her, he tilted his head as if remembering something.

"Have I met you before?" he asked. He also turned toward his godchildren for clarification.

"This is Red Watson, Papa," said Tilly, "and that's Claire, William, and Bailey."

Red's group waved at him awkwardly.

Mr. Ivansgrove smiled. "Oh, of course! My mind doesn't work the way it used to." He then peered toward the far back of the store, at the room he had just come out of. "Come on out, children. There is someone you may want to meet!"

Red tensed up. She gave Claire a look and was given the same look back.

"His grandchildren, I hear, are very fond of you," said Tilly.

Pretty soon, two little children came waddling out of the room. They stared at Red and then ran straight at her. They asked so many questions and were speaking over each other that Red couldn't hear a word they were saying.

"Calm down, calm down!" said Mr. Ivansgrove. "Only one question per minute."

One of the children looked up at Red. His eyes were wide and full of childlike innocence. "Do you really know how to shoot a bow and arrow?"

Red nodded. "My aunt taught me."

The other child, a girl, looked up at Red. Her face was small, and most of it was plastered with a giant smile. "Have you met Mr. Stone?"

Red nodded again. "Yes. Twice, actually."

The children gasped simultaneously, and Red couldn't help but laugh, this time, with her own giant smile. Mr. Ivansgrove placed a hand on both of his grandchildren's shoulders.

"Alright, that's enough." He smiled warmly. "We must get you two back to your parents."

The children rushed out with their grandfather, but the little girl ran right back to Red, who bent down to meet her eyes.

"Please be the reason my family lives," the girl said. Her eyes were steady this time, and she didn't stutter. She gave Red a hug and then ran back to Mr. Ivansgrove.

Red had no words, no way of explaining that particular feeling she couldn't quite grasp. She couldn't figure out if it was a good or bad sensation—or both. And it was those hard-to-reach feelings that got to her the most.

—m—

The foursome, led by Tilly and Ben, reached a fountain in the middle of the town center. Tilly explained that this was where Eleanor wanted them to wait for her.

Red looked around, but she couldn't find her aunt anywhere. She looked down at her hands, which were freezing cold.

"One moment," she said. Then she disappeared into the crowd.

She could almost hear Eleanor's voice, who was, at the moment, near a large tree. She ran a little quicker and eventually reached Eleanor, Peter, and Oliver, who were standing near a tall oak tree with a very distinctive carving at the center. It was of a sun, and its rays were definitely the main focus. There were also carvings of three letters under it: *E*, *A*, and *C*.

"Aunt Eleanor!" said Red, out of breath. She hugged her aunt. Then she noticed that Eleanor had a look in her eye that Red had never seen before.

"What are you doing here by this tree?" she asked.

Eleanor had dirt all over her dress and apron, though she attempted to hide it. "I may have discovered something astonishing that could change everything."

Red eyed the tree and then her aunt. "Well, it is a beautiful tree, but I don't know if—"

"Not the tree, dear," Eleanor interrupted. "What secrets the tree holds are what I'm searching for. I've tried everything, including placing a hand on the bark, but nothing has happened."

Red looked at the tree. She circled it slowly.

"Well, I don't see anything out of the ordinary," she said. She was slightly worried that she would disappoint her aunt.

Eleanor sighed and placed a muddy hand on her forehead. "This is ridiculous. What was I thinking? Let's just head back, dear."

Red decided not to ask Eleanor any follow-up questions. She picked up her bow, which she had left on the grass, and followed her aunt, Peter, and Oliver.

As they left, Red felt something different, like the tree knew something she didn't. She quickly let go of the thought, but it was like a stubborn rash and didn't leave.

—⚏—

"Alright, is everyone comfortable?" asked Eleanor from across the hall of a visitor's cottage their group was staying at.

"Yes, Aunt Eleanor," they stated unanimously.

"Very good," said Eleanor, retreating into her own room. "If any of you need anything just knock on my door."

Red shared a room with Claire, who snored louder than the shriek of a night corpse. She attempted to fall asleep but was unsuccessful even though her bed was extremely comfortable. She wondered why she was stopping herself from surrendering to sleep. She turned on her side to view Claire. An idea twisted its way into her mind as she kept her gaze on her sister as she made sure Claire was deeply asleep.

Red slowly pushed the covers away and stood up from her bed. She carefully made her way to the door and closed it sensibly behind her. Her footsteps were unbelievably loud and, at the moment, seemed almost louder than Claire's snoring.

Outside, it was freezing, but Red was prepared this time. She wore a large coat and carried a lantern. She sprinted in the dark and surprised herself on how nimble she was. But as soon as she reached a hill covered with grass and flowers, she stopped to catch her breath.

She looked up to see the tree with the sun silhouette carved on it, and she smiled.

For Aunt Eleanor, she thought to herself.

It took a notably hard time figuring out what to do first. She still had no clue why Eleanor was so interested in this tree. She stared at the sun carving and then at its rays. She almost felt compelled to place a hand on it.

But Aunt Eleanor already tried that, she thought. Still, she did the same anyway.

For a solid minute, nothing seemed to change. But before the waiting hit two minutes, the sun engraving started glowing a fantastic gold. Red quickly pulled back her hands, afraid the glowing would burn them. But she didn't feel any pain, just wonder.

Red watched as an area of the tree opened to reveal a staircase going down. They were steep enough to throw a stone down without it hitting the stairs. Red grabbed a smooth rock and threw it into the shadows. It took about two seconds before she heard a *clunk*.

"About sixty feet." Her voice echoed in the night.

Red felt nervous, especially because of her luck with mysterious staircases. Nonetheless, she was determined to discover what "secrets" her aunt was talking about. She headed down the stairs, watching her steps.

The walls were made of dirt, with the occasional root sticking out at the side. Red's lantern wasn't enough to light everything, so she feared each step as she continued into the unknown. The dirt walls had turned into bedrock as she finally reached a door made of dirt. She stopped to stare at it.

"I am not liking this," she mumbled.

She carefully opened the doorknob, and small pieces of dirt flew from the door. She had to push it with all her might to make it open. When it eventually opened, she found herself alone with the terrifying darkness surrounding her.

She lifted her lantern up and saw two other lanterns. She used her lantern to light the other two and create a lantern pattern that spread in a line across the whole room. She didn't understand it but was mesmerized by it.

Red stood in awe as the room lit up around her. There were many bookshelves—enough that it could be considered a library. Even with the walls of bedrock, the large room was incredible. Red started walking deeper into the room, which turned out to be one of many. She wondered if anyone still lived here and how they would react to her breaking in.

It must be a gifted, she thought. *If it wasn't, then they wouldn't use the gifted way of getting inside.*

Red smiled and started exploring the other side of the room. There was a small circular table with many scrolls piled up into a tower on it. There was an open scroll with writing that Red found interesting.

I have been here for many years. I am getting older and more afraid. I wonder every day if my decision was correct. It haunts me. Should I have left? Did I have any more to give? Maybe so, but it's already too late for me. I have disappointed my friends and family—and Mr. Stone. But there might be some hope for me left. Hopefully, I'll find the courage to see it.

—AW

"AW? What does that stand for?" Red mumbled.

"Well, I'm not really sure, but what I do know is that you have trespassed into my home," said a stern voice from behind her.

Chapter

Seventeen

Red dropped the scroll, which fell onto the floor. She picked it up anxiously and started making her way toward the entrance.

"I'm sorry. I'll just leave—wait, AW? Does that stand for Arthur Wildur?"

The man just stood there for a few seconds. He was Eleanor's age and had auburn-gray hair and a short beard. He looked tired but rested. Red couldn't tell whether he was good or bad just yet.

"Arthur," said the man quietly, "Wildur. Yes, that does sound familiar."

"Did he write these scrolls?"

"I'm sorry, but I just don't remember. Please, just leave." He had a look of fear in his eyes.

Red wondered why he was so anxious about visitors. But in his defense, she wasn't exactly invited.

She continued to the door. "Aunt Eleanor will be disappointed," she said under her breath.

"Wait," said the man. "Did you say Eleanor? Eleanor . . . I know that name."

Red quickly walked back toward him. "My aunt, Eleanor Watson. Do you know her?"

The man sat down, holding his head. He rummaged through the scrolls and found a particular scroll that looked older than time itself. He opened it and read it with intensity. Then he dropped it and looked straight at the wall in front of him. He walked toward Red, looking directly into her eyes.

"How is she?" he asked. His voice quivered as his eyes started welling up with tears.

"She's alright. But who are you? I promise I won't tell anyone your identity if you don't want me to." Red needed to know why Eleanor was so interested in that tree and if this man had anything to do with it. But she feared that he was a night corpse or someone else that was working for Callum.

"I swear to you I would tell you if I could remember. But I've been here for so long, alone with my mind, which is failing me."

"Maybe I can help you remember something else." Red wanted to help her aunt. But she wasn't sure why this man, who didn't remember anything, was the apparent "secret."

"Alright then, but I doubt anything will work," he said, seemingly forgetting that Red had intruded into his home.

"You seem to know my aunt Eleanor. Do you know anything about Callum?"

The man grabbed his head. He looked stressed. "Eleanor. Callum."

Red stood up; she was a little worried. The man stood up as well. He looked stressed, like his mind wouldn't let him remember but his heart needed to know.

After a few more questions about his family and friends, the man finally lifted his head in reliance.

"I remember . . ." he said quietly. "I remember the trees as they danced beautifully in the wind. I remember the sun, the clouds, and the sky as they would ever so softly cry upon the valleys of flowers. I remember laughter and bliss, as they provided me with many joyous memories. I remember my family and my friends. I remember Callum, the treacherous prince! I remember Mr. Stone, my friend with the warm eyes and smile. And I remember the lovely Eleanor, my lady with the gilded heart. I remember myself, a memory I kept locked away, for I feared what I would see. Now I stand here awake, standing upon the hallowed halls of guilt and redemption. I am Arthur Wildur."

Red grinned in awe, though she was not sure what to say. Arthur picked up the scroll from the ground. He held it against his heart as he sang a quick song that Red guessed was in gifted speech.

"So you're Arthur Wildur?" she asked, still in shock.

It was Arthur's turn to smile. "Yes, I am. Now that my mind is slowly healing, I must tell you. You are the answer we've all been waiting for. You see, this door only opens for the 'one,' as it said in a scroll I wrote a long time ago. You are the one, the one who will save us all!"

Red looked down. "Everyone is telling me that, and my heart wants to believe. But my head is doubting it more by the minute."

"What I've learned is that if you only let your head lead, then your view of the world will never be as beautiful. I wish I learned that a long time ago," Arthur said almost sheepishly.

"You know you can't live down here forever," said Red.

"Of course, I can, but in this case, where you mean 'shouldn't,' then I must firmly disagree with you, dear." Arthur had a sip of tea. "After everything that had happened, there isn't anything left for me—nothing I care about anymore."

"What about your family? And Aunt Eleanor and Mr. Stone?"

"Oh, they wouldn't fancy seeing me after all these years. Please don't tell them. I left, remember?" Arthur looked ashamed. "Besides, I like solitude. It gives me room to think."

"It's not healthy to live in your mind all the time," started Red, who felt pity for him, "and I'm sure Aunt Eleanor and Mr. Stone would be very happy to see you. Aunt Eleanor had been searching near that oak tree for something. I bet she was looking for you!"

Arthur turned his head. "Really?" he said. Then he quickly walked toward a bookshelf. "Never mind." He gave Red a genuine smile. "Thank you."

Red smiled and started to make her way through the dirt door and up the stairs. Her heart sank more and more with each step. She wished she could help him see that Aunt Eleanor and Mr. Stone did want to see him.

As she reached the tree, she realized that it was nighttime, and she almost stumbled back down the stairs.

She made her way back to the visitor's cottage. Her room was extra cold, and Claire's snores were extra loud. Red rolled her eyes as she watched her sister drool a little. She crawled back into bed as silently as she could just as the door swung open and a tired Will walked in, rubbing his eyes.

"What is it?" whispered Red. "Don't wake Claire up.

"I couldn't sleep," he said drowsily. "I kept thinking I heard footsteps or something."

Red pursed her lips. "Well, I'm sure it was nothing. Just go back to sleep. It'll be morning before you know it." She tried her best to smile, though she was having a hard time keeping her eyes open.

Will nodded and left. Red lay down and fell asleep just as her head hit the comfortable pillow.

—⚋—

It was morning, and Red woke up to birds chirping and the savory smell of Eleanor's cooking. She sat up in her bed and yawned and then looked over to Claire's bed. Her sister was lying diagonally on her bed with her feet on her pillow. Red got up and walked downstairs.

Eleanor stood in the kitchen with an already cooked breakfast. "Morning, dear," she said. "Fresh tattie scones and toast on the table."

Red sat uncomfortably in her chair—not because the chair was uncomfortable, but because she knew information Eleanor might have been searching for. Red ate a scone, but she couldn't stomach it, which was a tad odd because it was brilliant. Eleanor eyed her niece; she always knew when Red was upset.

"Something troubling you, dear?" Eleanor placed a few more plates on the table for the rest.

Red used her fork to poke a few holes in her scone. "It's nothing. I'm just tired."

Eleanor wasn't convinced, but she didn't push. Claire, Will, and Bailey came downstairs. They also looked tired, especially Will. Red looked down, feeling sick.

"Hey, what's up with you?" asked Will, yawning as he spoke. "You look like you caught the flu or something."

Red sighed as she lay back in her chair. "It's really nothing. I'm just tired."

After breakfast, Eleanor wanted everyone in the library for research, which was the real reason they went to Wildur.

They entered the library.

Mr. Ivansgrove sat in a chair, reading a novel. He smiled when he spotted Red and the rest.

"Why, hello again!"

"Good morning," Eleanor said in greeting. "My name is Eleanor, and they are—"

"I know who they are. My godchildren introduced me to them." He walked over to them and dropped a book into Will's hands: *Gifted Creatures* by Henry Ivansgrove.

"Did you write this, Mr. Ivansgrove?" asked Will.

"No, no, I love books, but I can't write even if I want to." Mr. Ivansgrove chuckled. "My eldest son wrote it. He works with incredible creatures, like the water fauna we have in Wildur."

The mention of Wildur made Red's stomach churn. Dark clouds started appearing, and pretty soon, it was drizzling. Mr. Ivansgrove walked over to the window, bewildered.

"How odd. It hasn't rained all year," he said under his breath.

Eleanor looked at her feet and then at her niece, who shot her an "I'm so sorry" look. Eleanor sighed and placed a hand on Red's shoulder, who rubbed her arm, embarrassed.

"Well, it helps the flowers grow, that's for sure," said Mr. Ivansgrove with a smile. "Now, what are you fellows looking for?"

Eleanor walked over to him and whispered something in his ear. He eyed her with a grim expression on his face.

"Follow me," he said.

They followed him deeper into the library. He stopped at a dusty shelf and felt the inside with his hand. Red thought it was some sort of button because as soon as he pressed it, a compartment appeared. Inside was a single scroll.

"This is the only thing we have on him," Mr. Ivansgrove said in a low voice as he unfolded it cautiously, "written by Mr. Wildur himself."

Eleanor placed a hand over her heart, and Red tried not to throw up from the churning of her stomach. Mr. Ivansgrove handed the scroll to Eleanor, who read it aloud, as quietly as she could.

My worries have only grown. My dear friend Charles Callum is showing signs of excessive fear and suspicion. Maybe I'm being paranoid, but I fear in my heart that he will soon not be himself entirely. When I discovered the Gifted Lands, I've always thought the gift to be a power any person would be exceptionally grateful to possess. But a power in this magnitude has its downfalls, and I am afraid that my friend has fallen under its spell. I am noticing a pattern when it comes to him. He fears courage, which means if you don't show any kind of mental weakness to his evil, he will see you as a threat—though a very small threat, to be precise. Another factor when it comes to being poisoned by power is blind self-admiration. He believes what he does is beneficial. He could very well be in deeper water. I am very disappointed. He was my best friend, and I will forever be haunted by this beautiful and terrible power that took a weak mind from its insignificant cage.

Silence.

Maybe silence was the better option, but Red never had any clue. Was it that hard to read someone's face? Or was there always the need for some sort of context clue or backstory to back up your inference? Nonetheless, the group stayed silent, and Red counted each second.

"I think it's best if we start packing our stuff," said Eleanor. It wasn't hard to read *her* face.

Red knew that they hadn't brought many belongings. She found it hard to swallow as mixed feelings swelled inside of her. They burned her insides.

They said their goodbyes to Mr. Ivansgrove, who could sense their discomfort. Then they went back to the cottage for a quiet evening.

Red wished she could read what Eleanor was thinking, though she longed and feared it. So she said nothing, which was sometimes the best and only thing one could do.

—⚶—

It was stormy outside, though not because of Red. She had already calmed down. She made that very clear to her siblings and Bailey after they accused her of bringing in the bad weather. Eleanor had made everyone hot tea, and they sat around the fireplace, telling stories. Red was glad how the night turned out, no matter how strange the day might have started.

"Alright, my turn," said Bailey. "You all never met me when you visited your aunt's house when you were younger because I would always hide since I was so nervous of outsiders." She got a look from Eleanor, who raised an eyebrow. "*And* I begged Ms. Watson to not tell you all about me so that you wouldn't try to look for me," she said, a little embarrassed.

Everyone laughed.

"My turn," started Will. "When I was five, I fell down a tree—and I use the term *fell* very loosely." He eyed his sisters.

"We did *not* push you down that tree. It was all your clumsy instincts, Will." Claire laughed.

Another round of laughter followed.

"Well, I do have *one* story," said Eleanor.

But she was interrupted by a short *knock* on the wooden door. Everyone turned, not knowing whether to be afraid or intrigued.

Eleanor stood up and looked out the window. She couldn't see anyone, but she opened the door anyways, thinking it was some sort of letter or something. As she opened it, she saw a cloaked man standing alone in the rain. Eleanor felt pity for him and let him in.

He took off his hood, and Eleanor nearly fainted.

Chapter

Eighteen

Shock. Silence.

Eleanor had been given a glass of water, but she wouldn't sit down. Her hand was on her chest, she could feel and hear her heart beating wildly. Red believed her aunt was both surprised and elated, but she was only half right.

"After all these years, you're here," started a teary-eyed Eleanor. She then seemed to switch emotions in the next second. "So what did running away and hiding do for you all these years?"

Arthur Wildur shifted his feet as he chose his words.

"Well, it's . . ." he started, but then he looked down at his feet. "You are right. You've always been. It was wrong to hide away for so many years. But please understand. It had nothing to do with you or—"

"Charles?"

Arthur hung his head. "I'm not going to lie to you, Eleanor."

Eleanor pursed her lips, but she eventually caved in. She gave her friend a long hug, and tears reappeared on her cheek.

Red was relieved. She smiled, and warm tears escaped her own eyes. She was glad Eleanor was happy. Then she felt something move on the table beside her. It was a flower with some dead petals around it. But the flower itself was not dead anymore. It started blooming and might have even grown a tad.

Red quickly wiped her eyes, not wanting anyone to see her cry. She picked up the flowerpot and showed it to her siblings.

Bailey gave her a reassuring look that said, "At least it's a good thing."

—∞—

It was foggy outside with a hint of unease. That was the best way Red could describe it. They had spent most of the night talking, yet none of them was even the slightest bit tired, especially with their unexpected houseguest.

Arthur sat uncomfortably. He felt ashamed but relieved. Eleanor still hadn't wrapped her head around everything. She was glad he was okay, but she still felt something deep inside that could make her cry out of anger.

"How are you?" Arthur asked Eleanor as he was handed a cup of tea by Bailey.

"Wonderful," Eleanor answered bluntly. "I am very glad to see you again, dear friend. But I do wonder one thing. You have been hiding from everything and everyone for many years. How did you accomplish that?"

"I did actually leave a way for others to find me," started Arthur. "I created a scroll that left a clue on my whereabouts."

"The old oak tree we used to love, yes, but I couldn't figure out anything else from the scroll. When I tried placing my hands on the tree, nothing happened."

"I had studied ways to make a lock with gifted unlocking abilities. I later found that it didn't work for any gifted except 'the one,' as I mentioned in the scroll. Your niece, being the one, was the only gifted able to enter," said Arthur.

Eleanor gave him a look and then turned to face Red. "You snuck out in the middle of the night?"

Silence.

"Yes, I did, and I'm sorry." Red hated the feeling of Eleanor being disappointed in her. It was a sort of feeling that would slide down your spine in a wave of guilt.

"She was also the one who gave me any hope. She's the reason I decided it was time to face the world again." Arthur gave Red an encouraging nod.

Eleanor sighed as she smiled. "Really? Well, that was good of her." She gave Red a warm smile, and Red took it gratefully.

"I do not fear you! What earth shall breathe its final breath shall not breathe it in vain! Show yourself!"

From the shadows of Tìr na h-Oidhche, the Land of Night, which lay restless along the borders of the sea, a man stood tall, sword in hand, holding his breath.

"I sense your fear. I breathe it in as air. You can't act strong forever, like that sword you have in your meager hand. It will soon rust over, an absolute waste of time," a voice countered from the shadows.

"If you're so confident that you have nothing to fear, then show yourself!" said the man, preparing his sword.

"I can't do that," replied the voice. "You see, I am part of the shadows. I *am* the shadows."

The man wasn't convinced.

"Come out into the light. It is not impossible." He stared deep into the darkness of the shadows. "By the order of the king!"

Mr. Stone circled the darkness, which seemed less frightening next to the light. He lifted his now-glowing sword. Then the source of the voice walked out into the light. He had the shape of man yet was only shadow.

Mr. Stone lowered his sword. "Follower of Callum, you will never win. The shadows have no chance against the light, which will burn the darkness into nothing. Evil fears it the most because it knows it will never win, which is why I wonder why it never sleeps."

Mr. Stone did not swing his sword, nor did he initiate a fight. He stood in his place, glaring. The shadow sent a wave of darkness toward Mr. Stone, who fell onto the sand. Lying on the ground, Mr. Stone reached for his sword.

The shadow laughed as he stared at him. "Your words are meaningless."

Mr. Stone could feel his sword with his fingers, though he did not grab it. He stood up, the palm of his hand glowing. He reached a hand out toward the shadow. A wave of light shot right out of it, burning the shadow and making it shriek in pain. Then the shadow turned to nothing.

Mr. Stone lay on his back, trying to catch his breath. His ribs hurt, and his head was spinning. He turned his head to look directly at Red.

—⁓—

Red sat up in a cold sweat. She grabbed her stomach and felt like throwing up. Her mind started to race, and her heart felt like it would explode out of her chest. She sat up in her bed, trying to control her heart rate.

Suddenly, she felt movement.

Her bed started shaking. Red quickly jumped off it and then realized it wasn't the bed that was shaking.

She had caused an earthquake!

She stood in the center of the room and extended her arms toward the two walls on either side of her. She didn't know how that would help, but she couldn't think of anything else at the moment. She could feel her arms tensing up as she used as much force as she could.

The ground stopped shaking, and Red fell to the ground. She stayed there until she caught her breath. Then she heard people rushing in.

Claire helped Red stand, and Eleanor looked at Red with wide eyes.

"What happened here, lass?" asked a frantic Eleanor.

"I had a dream that Mr. Stone was fighting this sort of shadow monster. At the end of it, Mr. Stone won, but he was on the ground. Then he looked directly at me with this look that . . . that I just can't explain." Red knew she sounded stressed, but she couldn't care less at the moment.

"So then you had to make an earthquake?" said Will anxiously and got a straight glare from Eleanor.

"Sit down on the bed, dear," said Eleanor. "William, go get her some water. Thank you, dear."

Will groaned but proceeded to fetch Red some water. Eleanor sat down on the bed next to Red and handed her a blanket.

"I am so proud of you, dear," she said with a warm smile, and Red looked up at her with confusion. Eleanor explained, "You were able to stop the earthquake on your own. That took courage, dear."

Red felt better. She gave Eleanor a hug, and the rest of the group joined in, even Will.

—∿—

"Alright, I know I made it a point to say that we wouldn't stay in Wildur for very long, but because of everything, we should wait a little until we get everything settled," Eleanor said. "Also, we need more information on Callum, and no other country will be as willing to help us."

Red tried her best to quell her excitement, though her efforts were easily recognized as pretentious. Eleanor grinned at her softly. Red felt happy but confused and a little scared. She still had many fears about the journey, but she knew how to deal with it—*mostly*.

Arthur also had a knowing grin on his face, but it was a bit unrecognizable, like he was planning something.

"Would you all fancy a visit to somewhere special?" he asked.

Eleanor smiled at him. "The garden? My heart longs to see it again, but my mind fears it will not be as magnificent as when I first laid eyes on it."

"If you only let your head lead, then your view of the world will never be as beautiful," said Red, repeating Arthur's words.

Arthur looked at her with pride.

Eleanor nodded. "Lead the way, Arthur." She smiled at him and her niece.

—∿—

Eleanor had packed a bag of apples and water, and she got a few remarks from Arthur about how she was "always so overprepared." Red laughed to herself. Eleanor and Arthur had everyone leave their weapons at the cottage, for they wouldn't need them, as Eleanor had told them.

"We aren't going to be attacked by night corpses or wolves or some other kind of terrifying monster, are we?" asked Will, which elicited groans of annoyance and embarrassment from Red, Claire, and Bailey.

Eleanor let out a small chuckle and proceeded to let everyone out the door. "Don't fret, William. The garden is special. I will explain to you all later."

And then they were gone. One by one, each stepped out the door with similar perspectives. Eleanor and Arthur felt excited. Red felt intrigued, and the rest of the group tried hard to calm Will down. Nevertheless, the road Arthur chose was lovely, and Red couldn't imagine anything bad happening.

Red watched her feet as she walked. "Before Arthur came, back at the visitors' cottage, you said you had a story to tell," she said to Eleanor, who caught her hint with delight.

"Yes, well, I was going to share a story about that tree with the sun engraving," she started. "We were a little older than you all, and it was the most beautiful day. A tree we had planted long ago stood before us."

It was a tree growing in time, bright or fearsome, calm or unsettling. While one person might feel a certain way, another might seek a different path. Three children lay their heads along the roots of the magnificent tree, each with unique thoughts wandering in and out of their innocent minds.

The girl played with a few strands of her golden brown hair. She wore a pale yellow dress with white lace on the edges. Her mind was filled with thoughts of joy and memories of her family. The boy next to her had auburn hair and a warm smile. He thought of better ways to help the country. And the third child, a boy with dark brown hair, had thoughts of power. He played with two leaves as he twisted them around then. Eventually, he ripped them apart without realizing it.

"Charlie, stop! Don't hurt the leaves," said the girl, hitting his arm gently.

Charles sighed. "Only you would ever say that." He smiled at her.

The boy with auburn hair looked up at the sky in wonder. He watched as the light rays hit a specific part of the tree. It looked like a swirl of the sunlight. He traced it with his fingers; it felt warm. Then he noticed that, unfortunately, the same spot was also rotting.

"It's so beautiful," he said. Then he eyed the rotting part curiously. "I have an idea." He grabbed his sword and started to cut into the tree.

Young Eleanor Watson eyed him. She had a horrified expression.

"Arthur! Seriously, what is with you two and destroying nature?" Eleanor then stopped and watched as Arthur cut only the rotting parts, using the sun as his guide.

Eventually, a magnificent carving of a sun was delicately engraved into the tree. The trio stared at it with awe.

Arthur handed Eleanor his sword. "All we need now is to leave our mark," he said with a smile.

Eleanor traced an *E* onto the tree and then handed the sword back to Arthur, who carved an *A*. Charles sighed. He was never one for sentimentality, but he reluctantly carved a sloppy *C*.

Eleanor placed her hands on the tree to make sure it was completely healed on the inside. She rested her hands on her dress as she felt a sense of calm washing over her.

"It's healed."

———✖———

"And that's the story of the tree and how we saved it while turning it into a timeless memory." Eleanor smiled at the memory.

Everyone had listened in silence. While it was a simple story, Eleanor told it in a way that felt special, and everyone genuinely loved it.

Arthur placed a hand over his heart. "So simple everything was that now my eyes start to tear up. What else intends to change before my withered eyes that I shall glow in despair? I say it not so. I will remember the best and the worst, though my heart will stay in confusion for how long I have not been told. It is a memory so sweet I will hold dearly. Thank you, Eleanor."

The rest of the group listened to the poetic words of Arthur Wildur, who now stood still, his eyes fixated on something just beyond the green pine trees. Eleanor placed a hand on her heart as she, too, looked in the same direction. The foursome could only watch in wonder.

Before their eyes was a brilliant garden.

Chapter

Nineteen

Golden—what other way could one describe something so magnificent? There were tall arches with vines of roses wrapped around them. There was every flower imaginable, and the stairs led up a hill of green and white. A lake with crystal clear water glowed under the light of the sun. All seemed as if it had never aged a day.

Eleanor picked a sunflower, Red's favourite flower, and placed it gently behind her niece's ear. Red felt it, though she was still deeply entranced by the garden. She wanted to lie in the grass for hours and climb the tallest trees. She didn't feel the need to be afraid or worried. She held on to her shoulders in shock and closed her eyes as tears welled up in them. The rest of the group were just as awed.

"Is this the Gifted Land Country?" asked Red.

Eleanor smiled. "In a way. We're still in Wildur, but this garden was a gift from the Gifted Land Country. It's our own small taste of genuine eloquence." Her smile was as light as a feather, though her words rang in elation.

For the rest of the day, they enjoyed the lovely, picturesque garden. The water from the lake felt warm from the sun, which provided it with a coat of shining glitter.

Red felt her heart, and this time, it was good. She decided to join her siblings, who were sitting near a row of sunflowers.

Then she suddenly felt something . . . odd.

Odd is good, she told herself.

But the feeling bit like frostbite down her spine. The wind blew her hair into her face, and her eyes stung.

She fell over onto the grass, and when she stood back up, the garden had turned into a deep gray and black. She couldn't feel her legs as she walked, and she didn't even know where she was going anymore. Her mind was evading her as the colour of the world seemed to melt away.

Then she heard footsteps. There were terrifying thumps on the grass as someone crept closer. Red wiped her hair out of her eyes; at the moment, her hair looked like a mess. She didn't want to look up. She didn't want to face anything or anyone. She was scared but didn't want to admit it.

"I know who you are," she said quietly.

Silence.

She waited for a response, and it felt like a year being trapped in a tight box. Red could feel the seconds tick by, which aligned perfectly with her pulse.

"Weak," said the voice. "What a waste of this incredible power."

Red looked up. She reached for her bow but realized she had left it at the cottage. She looked into the eyes of Callum, who carried a sword. She let out a small gasp. She didn't want to look at him, at his red eyes, torn flesh, and wicked smile.

"Let me guess. You are not afraid of me?" he said, which was answered with a firm nod from Red. "What do you know about power? What do you know about fear? Look at me. You think I want to look like this?" Callum's voice was unnerving. "You think you know what darkness is? You think you have it all figured out, don't you?"

Red clenched her fists, and small cracks appeared in the ground. Callum eyed them, and a hint of fear sprouted in his heart. But he was great at hiding it.

"You don't know anything about me, child," he continued, turning his head.

At that moment, Red suddenly felt a terrible ache in her stomach. Then she screamed in pain. Her stomach felt like it was on fire. She fell to the ground and clutched the nearest patch of grass.

Callum stayed still. Red grabbed at her stomach but eventually found the strength to stare up at his cold, dead eyes.

"I am not afraid of you," she said even as burning tears escaped her eyes.

Callum turned his head, so it was straight again. Red released her hand from her stomach, which instantly stopped burning. She still kept a good grip on the patch of grass.

"Back at Elivar," she started, though her voice was dry and wavering, "why did you make one of your night corpses go instead of you?"

"Well, I was busy," he said in the most cocky way. "Besides, my night corpses could easily trick the queen into believing her plan was sensible. They even planted the seed in her head."

"Weren't you afraid the night corpse would talk and ruin your awful plan?"

"Everyone has a hard time betraying me." He threw his sword onto the ground. "I won't need this."

Red glared at his sword. She still couldn't catch her breath.

"You won't win. I know your weakness," she said, remembering the scroll from Mr. Ivansgrove's shop.

"I could say the same about you," said Callum.

"You're afraid of yourself. You're afraid of anyone showing courage against you," said Red calmly.

Callum stayed silent. His eyes were large and red. He slowly lifted his right arm.

Red screamed again. This time, from her right arm came waves of pain. She lay on the grass, grabbing her shoulder. Callum looked down at her. Then he brought his arm all the way above his head.

Crack.

Red screamed louder. She knew her arm was broken, but she hated showing any weakness to Callum. She gritted her teeth. She wondered if he was afraid of her because he knew she was a threat. *He* was weak.

"All my life, I knew it was me. I bet Arthur told you to listen to your heart. Well, my heart lied to me. My father looked me in the eye and told me I was capable of great things, that I was the one. I trusted everyone, and now they all say it was my doing that turned me into this. I look like fear because I didn't accept it as a part of life. Fear will stop you if you don't embrace it fully. Look at me. I accepted the fact that we gifted people will bring prosperity, and if this is the way to accomplish that, then so be it."

Red was only half-listening. She could feel sweat pouring down her face. Callum picked a flower from the ground. It was a beautiful flower, soft yellow. But as soon as it was touched by Callum, it shriveled up and died. He turned to view Red.

"You see this?" He ripped the flower up and threw it near her. "This is what I am—a monster." He kneeled down to look directly at Red. "And you will be one too."

"No!"

Callum disappeared, leaving Red on the cold dirt.

She closed her eyes, trying hard not to shed a tear. She then realized that her arm felt fine. She straightened it out and saw that it wasn't broken. Red raised her eyebrows.

"It was all in my mind," she said in shock.

Eleanor quickly ran over to her, followed by the rest of the group.

"What happened here, dear?" she asked.

Red stood up slowly. "You didn't see him?"

They shook their heads.

"If anyone was here, I would have found them already," said Bailey, transforming back into her human form.

"Still waiting for my question to be answered, dear," said Eleanor, a look of worry plastered on her face.

Red blinked frantically. "He was here. Callum was here! He broke my arm, but it was actually all in my head. Then he told me I was going to become like him."

Eleanor placed a hand on her niece's shoulder and looked her in the eyes. Her arm was firm and strong, and it almost felt like a hug.

"Never listen to Callum. He is worse than night corpses when it comes to fooling the mind. Everything will be alright. He knows that you are strong, so he's just trying to use that against you," said Eleanor, though she knew there was nothing she could say to protect her niece's mind from Callum's evil. Still, she meant what she said.

"Let's head back," said Eleanor, giving her niece a big hug.

—⁓—

Red sat underneath a tall oak tree. It had been a couple of days since her encounter with Callum, and she replayed everything over and over in her head. Paranoia kept her busy—she hated that the most. In her hands, she held her bow and the flower Eleanor had placed behind her ear. These were the only things that could bring her comfort at the moment.

She listened to the sounds of nature. She felt different. She knew she had to stay strong. She knew fear, and she knew courage. The tide between both was strong and kept pushing her into both oceans. She felt nothing as she felt everything. Her spirit was lifted as her mind felt weak.

A curious light shone through the branches of the trees above her, and she spotted the dove perched on one of the branches. It seemed to be smiling down at her. That did it. It gave her the comfort she so desperately needed.

But a certain feeling still invaded her soul. It was strong yet barely noticeable, and it burned her heart like cold iron.

End of Book One

Acknowledgements

To the reader, I thank you for reading my novel. Since I'm still a kid, I don't have extensive professional writing experience, but I am very fond of writing and language, which I believe is my motivator for writing a novel. Something about creating characters and an intricate storyline is incredible to me, and I wanted to try it for myself. I have always dreamed of writing a book for the sole reason of making a difference with my words. Hopefully, this novel will make someone smile. I truly appreciate all the support, and I hope you enjoyed reading it as much as I enjoyed coming up with it and writing it.

Thanks to my family for, as I said before, dealing with me, especially Dad and Mom and my cats—Char, Ari, and Precious.

Thanks to my incredible friends for loving me as I am and for always making me laugh.

Quotes from My Family

What an amazing thing, watching her creative artistic drive flourish in written form.

—Dad

Watching you grow and achieve your dreams fills our hearts with pride and joy. Your creativity never ceases to amaze me. I love your self-confidence and determination to follow your dreams. May you always keep these qualities that make you who you are. Always remember that you are enough. We love you not because of your accomplishments but because you are our precious daughter. May your spirit keep shining bright always. God bless you!

—Mom

Quotes from My Crazy, Wonderful Friends (Alphabetized by Last Name)

She always sees the bright side of things.
—SC

A person who knows all the *Lord of the Rings* quotes.
—MF

She went from loving books to writing them.
—EP

Her magnificent mind charms me.
—RR

She is too smart.
—AS

She couldn't have done it without her beautiful personality.
—IS

I knew you could do it! Of course, couldn't have done it without us and most importantly, your cats.
—LT

So proud of you, LJ! You've worked so hard, and I can't wait to see what the future has in store for you.
—LT

Don't worry about what others think. They're just jealous.
—MV

9 798888 109861